Fetterman relaxed, then squeezed the trigger

The firing pin clicked, but nothing else happened. Quickly he cranked the bolt open and jacked another round into the chamber.

"Here's one for Staff Sergeant Henry Roland," he said, then squeezed the trigger again. The gun cracked and a moment later a sharp white flash of light blotted out the truck. Shredded canvas, wooden bows and jagged pieces of metal wrenched from the ZIL blew out in all directions, cutting down trees and bushes. A cloud of dust obscured their vision, and a few moments later the shock wave buffeted the helicopter.

When the dust cleared, Fetterman could clearly see a gigantic crater gouged out of the earth where the ZIL once stood. All around the crater were further signs of devastation. A circle of trees closest to the blast had been turned into kindling, and a little beyond that the vegetation had been knocked flat.

"Jesus!" Umber exclaimed. "Looks like an A-bomb hit it."

Gerber grinned. "Here's one situation where we can't get a body count. Best we could do is a body-part count."

VIETNAM: GROUND ZERO.

SPIKE

ERIC HELM

A GOLD EAGLE BOOK FROM
WORLDWIDE.

TORONTO · NEW YORK · LONDON · PARIS
AMSTERDAM · STOCKHOLM · HAMBURG
ATHENS · MILAN · TOKYO · SYDNEY

First edition October 1990

ISBN 0-373-62726-2

Printed in U.S.A.

VIETNAM: GROUND ZERO.

SPIKE

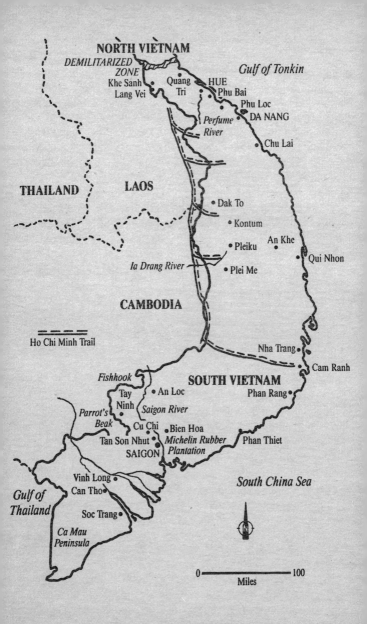

PROLOGUE

OCTOBER 1967 SANTA CRUZ, BOLIVIA

The killers waited patiently to spring their deadly trap. Special Forces Staff Sergeant Henry Roland and the eleven other members of his operational detachment A-team were concealed throughout the tangle of bushes and trees that made up the jungle's landscape. Their positions roughly described an X and effectively covered a fifty-foot length of the well-traveled trail. Once the shooting started, every living creature in the kill zone would risk annihilation.

The twelve Special Forces troopers had been waiting since before dawn. In total silence the men lay prostrate in the dirt, their faces painted black-and-green, black baseball caps pulled down low over their eyes. Similarly all the weapons were painted nonreflective black so that an errant glint of sunlight wouldn't inadvertently provide a warning. Immersed in the bush in this manner they were invisible to the human eye and very nearly invisible to the legions of howler monkeys, parrots and other tree-dwelling creatures.

Roland was close to six feet tall and two hundred pounds. He knew he was different from most men. Even though he was a team player in the SF, essentially he was loner. But then again, it took a different kind of emotional makeup to be a blaster. And no matter how you cut it, being a Green Beret demolition man was a strange occupation. Roland wiped the river of sweat off his forehead, wishing he had been born in the early 1800s in the Wild West so that he could have been a mountain man. Even better, he should have been born centuries ago, back in the days of the Mongol hordes.

To pass time and dispel the nagging boredom, Roland did what he always did whenever duty compelled him to run a direct-action mission—he daydreamed about long-legged, ample-breasted women. His mind's eye transported him to the familiar sidewalks and streets of Colón, the port town in Panama just outside the Eighth Special Forces Group headquarters at Fort Gulick. Sergeant Roland's favorite hangout in downtown Colón was the Club Trópico, a seedy tavern where girls imported from Colombia cheerfully worked the oldest profession in the world.

Judging from the ravishing beauties Roland had seen at the Club Trópico, he believed the Colombian ladies to be the most attractive and charming women in the world. Ravishing beauties or not, a roll in the hay cost a mere five dollars or the rough equivalent of five icy bottles of Balboa beer. Even better than the rock-bottom price, there was no pretense of love involved in the sex-for-money transaction. And if you didn't want to, you didn't even have to make small talk with the women afterward.

Roland passed the time in this manner, recalling all of the different working girls he had bedded in Panama. There had been Alicia, Julia, Maria and Anna. Some had been tall, some short, some well endowed, others less buxom. Out of all of his conquests, Anna had been the best, he concluded, pausing to luxuriate in the memory of her. Just thinking about the sensual woman quickened his pulse. He lingered over the lusty memories—the long, gentle curve of her breasts, her full ruby red lips, the special look that came over her face whenever she eased him onto the bed and then climbed on top of him. He felt his penis growing hard against his thigh, recalling how her long black hair cascaded down her shoulders and brushed his face, remembering how it felt to thrust against her and how she had tasted when he kissed the sweat beaded on her brow....

Roland forced himself to stop the exquisite form of self-torture. How long had it been since he had been with a woman? For this mission they had been cooped up in the isolation phase for nearly a week, by necessity entirely cut off from the outside world while they digested all of the pertinent geographic and political information. Memorizing the names of the mayor and prominent merchants, the layout of the road, valleys and mountain trails was a serious business. Since they weren't allowed to carry maps or notes, everything had to be committed to memory. Roland's team had actually been on the ground and in position for another week. That meant the last time he had lain with a woman had been... Roland decided it was longer than he cared to think about.

A twig snapped somewhere down the trail. Startled out of his reverie, he mentally shifted gears and prepared for the day's inevitable violent outcome. After what seemed like interminable hours of immobility and silence, the payoff appeared to be within earshot. Was their quarry approaching, unaware of the trap that had been set? Roland strained his ears and could faintly hear the sound of voices jabbering away in Spanish about a woman, her easy virtue and her special skills at pleasing a man's appetite for love. Love and lust, mused Roland, the common thread that binds and blinds all men.

Roland wiped his shirtsleeve across his eyes and then his forehead, sponging up so much sweat that his sleeve came away drenched. Next he checked his weapon for the umpteenth time, making sure it was cocked. On this direct-action mission, he and all of the other team members were carrying Belgian-made FN-FAL rifles chambered for 7.62 mm NATO-specification rounds. By design and special arrangement, there were no serial numbers stamped on the weapons. Similarly they wore patchwork uniforms comprised of German hiking boots and Aussie camous. By virtue of the hodgepodge clothing and equipment, they were effectively sterile and unable to be traced back to any particular country. That way, if they flubbed the mission, no politicians would be embarrassed by the identification of corpses. No one, that is, except for the team proper and their bereaved next-of-kin.

But then Roland had no intention of failing this assignment by getting himself killed. Direct-action missions were his specialty, and he had been very successful at them for more than two years. The Green Beret sergeant was confident this action would go the same way.

The man they were stalking, known as El Doctor, was a serious troublemaker who organized guerrilla bands that, in turn, terrorized the countryside, burning peasant huts and murdering unsympathetic farmers, their wives and little children. If all went well, the good doctor would soon be shoveling coal in hell.

Roland lined up the sights on the enemy point man, secure in the knowledge that if he squeezed the trigger slightly, a bullet would slam into the man's forehead and cancel his existence. Instead of firing, though, he let the guerrilla soldier pass by without harm. Roland had always wondered how it would feel to be on point and walk blissfully past an ambush only to have it erupt into a firefight behind your back. Would you feel dreadfully stupid because you missed the telltale signs, or simply count your blessings and feel selfishly lucky?

Moments later a second man walked up the trail and into view, soon followed by a third and a fourth. Finally Roland saw the reason the A-team had traveled so far and gone to so much trouble.

The target was wearing his three distinctive trademarks: a black beret, a scruffy beard and an unlit Cuban cigar clenched between his teeth. The Communist guerrilla leader was nicknamed El Doctor by his followers because he had supposedly attended medical school in Mexico City. But Roland believed otherwise. The CIA dossier contradicted the guerrilla leader, insisting he had been a college dropout who read voraciously. A good bullshitter, the file claimed, a man who could convince a nonexpert he knew what he was talking about. Either way, reasoned Roland, the doctor was about to shake hands with the devil.

The Special Forces sergeant took a deep breath, let out half of it and waited for the inevitable moment when one of his partners froze time by triggering a claymore mine, the one item of American manufacture they had brought with them. In the meantime, Roland trained his sights on the good doctor's cigar, intently watching as the doomed man chomped on it.

The team commander detonated the claymore, which erupted with a sharp, resounding bang, its explosive charge scattering hundreds of steel pellets down the length of the trail. The fusillade was like a huge sword, cutting a wide swath through men, tree branches and leaves, knocking down everything in its path.

When the pellets clawed at his body, El Doctor's face took on a stunned expression. His knees buckled and he toppled facedown onto the ground, raising a cloud of dust.

Roland figured the doctor was dead before the dust settled. But he had learned the hard way never to count on such things. He squeezed the trigger, firing off a 3-shot burst into the fallen guerrilla leader. The body jerked as the bullets tore into it, and blood began to ooze from dozens of holes until a red puddle formed beneath the belly and spread outward.

Roland turned his attention to the other guerrillas. Out of the twenty-man party, eighteen had been killed outright by the claymore. "Teach the sorry bastards to bunch up like that," muttered the sergeant. The two guerrillas left alive were wounded but that didn't stop them from firing back. One man hid behind a tree and the other took refuge behind a truck-sized boulder. Now we'll see what they're made of, Roland thought, knowing their only escape from the predicament was to charge headlong into the heart of the ambush and try to break out. He doubted they would do that, though. He had seen this situation dozens of times before. Roland was pretty certain the enemy guerrillas would choose to die like rabbits huddled in their nest.

The Green Beret sergeant's rifle bolt locked back, empty. He grabbed two 5-shot stripper clips out of his ammo pouch, reloaded and worked the bolt to lock and load a round. By the time he finished, the battleground had fallen deathly silent. All of the small-arms fire had stopped, which meant the last of the guerrillas had either run out of ammunition or blood.

Roland got to his feet and warily walked toward El Doctor's body, but he stopped dead in his tracks a full five yards away. One of the other SF troopers ran up beside him, intent upon checking the dead guerrilla leader's body. Roland stuck out an arm and held the man back. "No wait," he cautioned. "Too many hunters have been killed by a downed tiger they thought was dead when it wasn't."

Roland raised his rifle, took careful aim and squeezed the trigger. When the bullet hit the dead doctor, it snapped his head back and opened up a 7.62 mm hole in the forehead. "Now we're pretty sure he's dead."

Solemnly the two of them walked the remaining few steps to the body. Gently Roland touched the dead man's chin and rolled the head over to get a clear look at the face. Positive ID, he noted. Next he sank to his haunches and started searching the corpse for ID cards, matchbooks, documents and maps, in short, anything that would provide intelligence data. But the job was complicated by the numerous shrapnel wounds, bullet holes and copious amounts of blood.

Nevertheless, Roland turned the pant pockets inside out, finding nothing more than lint. It was almost the same story in the shirt pockets, with one exception. El Doctor was carrying a cheap black ballpoint pen. Somehow it had survived the hail of fire unscathed.

Roland plucked the souvenir out of the dead man's pocket and held it out in front of him. He clicked the button repeatedly, revealing the hidden nib. Finally he stuck the pen into his own pocket and growled, "To the victor belong the spoils."

Five minutes later the team was heading for the LZ and extraction.

1

JUNE 1968 TAN SON NHUT AIRPORT SAIGON, RVN

They were flying hell-bent three or four feet off the deck, racing for a huge gap in the tree line about a klick in front of the helicopter. Once they passed through the trees, the Huey popped back up to five hundred feet, banked left and then lost altitude again, coming to a hover a couple of feet off the ground.

A split second before the skids touched down at Tan Son Nhut, Master Sergeant Anthony B. Fetterman threw open his seat belt buckle and hunched forward in the troop seat, poised to exit the aircraft cargo door. If he had a quarter, he mused, for every time he had landed at the Hotel Three helipad, he could buy a round of beers for every ground-pounder in-country, even the straight legs.

As usual the flight from the A-Detachment near the Cambodian border had been uneventful. Fetterman considered the milk runs to MACV Headquarters the rough equivalent of a bare-bones R and R. Usually the pilot flew at fifteen hundred feet, an altitude safely above small-arms range. Fetterman reasoned it was one of the few times he could relax and not worry about stopping a bullet or a barrage of mortar fragments. He used such flights to catch his breath and redefine sanity in the midst of a crazy war.

Like the war itself, Fetterman was something of an enigma. Diminutive and olive-skinned, with close-cropped black hair and dark eyes, he didn't look anything like a stereotype of a combat soldier. Instead, from a distance, he could easily be someone who made his living selling Bibles or encyclopedias door-to-door. But up close that image faded fast. The hardness in his eyes strongly suggested that he was one man who meant whatever he said and was prepared to back it up with maximum force. Fetterman knew more ways to kill a man than most soldiers had years.

Now the master sergeant felt a mild jolt as the chopper's skids bumped the grassy field. At that precise moment he and his two companions grabbed their M-16s and rucksacks and leaped out onto the grass. Without hesitating, they ran in a crouch toward the terminal building. Once clear of the rotor wash, the three men pulled green berets out of their jungle fatigues pant pockets and placed them on their heads, yanking and twisting the headgear until they were properly positioned with the Fifth Special Forces flashes centered immediately above their left eyes.

Staff Sergeant Henry Roland stared a couple of hundred yards away from Hotel Three where he could see a U.S. Air Force F-86 fighter jet proudly displayed like a World War II tank or artillery piece in the middle of a town square. "You guys ever work with this spook before?" he asked.

Roland had been in-country for more than a month. Unlike other SFers who were newly arrived from Fort Bragg or Bad Tolz, West Germany, he'd had no problem acclimatizing to South Vietnam's tropical heat and humidity, not after spending a three-year tour with an A-team assigned to the Eighth Special Forces Group in the Panama Canal Zone deep in the heart of the jungle.

"Worked with Maxwell plenty of times," Captain MacKenzie K. Gerber said absentmindedly. "Hey, I think that's our jeep waiting over there." He pointed at a vehicle parked just outside the chain-link fence and gate where a Green Beret driver sat on the hood, reading a *Playboy* magazine. The pages were spread wide open to show the length and breadth of the centerfold. Abruptly the three men changed direction and started walking toward the *Playboy* reader.

Roland pressed the point. "So what's this guy Maxwell like?"

Fetterman offered his appraisal. "He's basically an okay guy. For a CIA type, anyway. He'll only lie to you or put your life in serious jeopardy if it's clearly in the line of duty, or in the best interests of his career."

Roland clucked his tongue. "I know the type. Worked with some of them with the Eighth. Never turn your back on them."

"Never been to Fort Gulick," Gerber said. "What kind of duty does the Eighth pull?"

Roland bit his lip before answering. "Oh, you know how it goes with those cushy country club assignments. Formation at 8:00 a.m., off duty at five. Weekends off for beachcombing or tarpon fishing. Once every couple of months you pull guard duty at the ammo dump so that the Panamanians don't break into one of the bunkers and blow themselves to kingdom come. You do rotations at the School of the Americas and teach Salvadoran, Chilean and Guatemalan soldiers how to set up a mortar base plate and barber poles. You know how it goes."

Fetterman pointed at the patch sewn on the bottom of Roland's right shirt pocket. On its blue circular background a white Spanish galleon sported a red Maltese cross in its sails. The words "Jungle Expert" were stitched along the bottom. "I see you've been to the jungle operations training center. You're a jungle expert.''

Roland shrugged. ''Yeah. Sometimes instead of guard duty we taught jungle warfare to American troops on their way over to Vietnam.'' Then he corrected himself. ''On their way over here, I mean.''

Fetterman nodded. ''Either way you shouldn't have any trouble acclimatizing to Vietnam's flora and fauna. Jungle is jungle.''

''Except there are no bushmasters or fer-de-lance to worry about in Southeast Asia,'' Roland added. ''They only grow those suckers in the Americas.''

Fetterman's eyes glistened. ''You're right. But we've got venom-spitting cobras, nasty black mambas and Charlie righteous Cong. Any one of those three would dearly love to sink their fangs into your ass.''

''This your first tour in Nam?'' Gerber asked.

''Yep. First time in-country,'' Roland replied. He hoped they didn't notice how the words caused a gallon of bile to raise in his stomach, how his jaw was so tightly clenched that he was barely able to force the words out. In the world of Special Forces, being maneuvered into admitting you'd never been to Vietnam was roughly akin to announcing you'd never been laid.

''No combat experience then,'' Fetterman said, summing it up.

Roland nearly chocked on his own answer. "Nope." Because his missions in Latin America had been top secret, he couldn't discuss any details. Ironically, during his tour in Panama, he'd repeatedly volunteered to serve in Vietnam. The reason was simple: he had accurately perceived that his career was in crisis. Other staff sergeants with less time in grade and less time in service were being promoted to platoon sergeant ahead of him, based on the fact that they had one or more combat tours with the Fifth in Vietnam.

Roland had no combat tour listed in his 201 file. This was a source of considerable frustration for Roland, since he and his A-team had been running direct-action, live-fire missions in Central and South America for three years. Because his hush-hush missions were classified, he couldn't tell anyone, which meant that, officially, no one, especially the promotion board, knew or could give him credit for what he had done. As a result, there were no medals for bravery, no credit for the coveted CIB, no credit for the combat parachute jumps he had made.

Fetterman wrapped an arm around Roland's shoulder and talked to him in a paternal voice. "Don't worry about how you'll do under fire. Just watch one of us. You'll catch on real quick. It can't be that much different from what you were teaching back in Panama, other than the live rounds cracking overhead, that is."

"You're right," Roland said. "Can't be that much different from what I'm used to."

Gerber added his support. "This tour can't help but improve your promotion points. You'll come away with at least a combat infantryman's badge."

"A CIB," Fetterman said wistfully. "Every young stud infantryman's dream."

"A CIB," Roland repeated, stifling his urge for sarcasm. "Yeah, I'd sure like to earn one of those. To finally see combat." He hoped the tone of his voice didn't betray his anger.

After a short, kidney-jarring ride in the jeep over to MACV Headquarters, they entered the building, descended a stairwell and walked down a corridor lined with cinder-block walls damp with condensation. Rust spots stained the floor tiles where metal chairs, tables and filing cabinets had once stood. Finally Gerber halted in front of a dark wooden door and knocked. "It's us, Maxwell," he said.

Jerry Maxwell was their case officer, the man who provided them with assignments and supporting intelligence data. Fetterman nudged Roland and whispered, "The one important thing to remember about Maxwell is that his work is so secret even he doesn't know what he's doing." A moment later the door swung open and they trooped into the room single-file.

Roland was the last one in, and he involuntarily took a step back. It looked as if a Vietcong's rocket-propelled RPG grenade had impacted and exploded in Maxwell's office. One wall was lined with a row of battleship-gray filing cabinets, one of which featured an impressive combination lock. Three of the four drawers on that cabinet were pulled wide open, and their combined weight threatened to tip the cabinet over. Similarly disarrayed, the top of Maxwell's desk was littered with dozens of file folders. A puddle of still-wet red liquid stained the floor where someone had clumsily spilled ink while attempting to refill a top-secret stamp pad. Dozens of Coke cans cluttered the desk as if standing guard over the classified documents. Because the office was below ground level and had no windows, the fluorescent lighting gave it an eerie glow. It was the kind of place where you couldn't tell what time it was without a clock. And even though the supercooled air from upstairs didn't filter down to the lower level, it was still considerably cooler in Maxwell's office than outside.

Fetterman casually walked over to the wall where a framed reproduction of *The Hayfield Fight* was tilted off-center. He straightened it, then walked back across the room to stand with the others.

Maxwell, a short, sunburned man, looked up at the three visitors, smiled and said, ''You're going north this time, and I'm sure that comes as no surprise to you. That is, after all the 'in' place to summer I'm told." Maxwell laughed at his own joke. "Though I'd prefer the French Riviera myself."

Neither Gerber, Fetterman or Roland laughed, and Maxwell either didn't notice their lack of reaction or just didn't care. In spite of his attempt at humor, the CIA man looked tired. His face was drawn and his black hair was damp and plastered against his forehead. With the dark circles under his eyes and stubble dotting his face, he looked utterly exhausted, as if he hadn't slept for days. His rumpled white suit hung on his gaunt figure as if it belonged to another man. It was obvious that the CIA man had lost at least twenty pounds in the tropical heat.

Maxwell motioned them into an array of folding wooden chairs positioned in front of his beat-up desk. Then he opened a can of Coke, took a long pull and set it on the desktop with all the others. As usual, he never bothered to offer his visitors coffee or cold drinks. Instead, he held up a handful of papers bound by a cover sheet stamped Top Secret. "You'll never guess what this is," he said in a conspiratorial tone.

"Let me make a wild guess," Fetterman responded sarcastically. "It's got something to do with the heathen Communists."

"And world domination," Gerber added, jabbing a finger into the air for emphasis.

Maxwell ignored the verbal abuse. His voice was ominously serious, "This material is so sensitive that it must never be compromised. With that in mind, I'm going to burn it right now with you three men present as witnesses."

Gerber and Fetterman exchanged puzzled glances, then watched as Maxwell crumpled the sheaf of papers and stuffed them into an ordinary manila envelope. "Borrow your lighter?" he asked Fetterman, holding out his hand.

The master sergeant purposely took his time burrowing into his pant pockets, pretending he couldn't find his lighter. When he was satisfied he had kept Maxwell waiting long enough, he finally pulled out his Zippo. "Ah, here it is."

Maxwell extended the document in Fetterman's direction. "You light it."

Fetterman shook his head and put the lighter in the CIA agent's free hand. "Thanks, but no thanks. I'm very careful never to destroy U.S. government property. No, I'll leave this operation in your eminently capable hands."

Maxwell deftly flipped open the Zippo and whirled the igniting wheel. Once lit, he held the flame inside the envelope. The contents starting burning instantly, the papers blackening and curling up. Then, without warning, the manila envelope flared dangerously. Maxwell's eyebrows rose for a millisecond. "Damn!" he said finally, hurling the ball of flame into the wastebasket.

With the fire already forgotten, he shook his singed hand in an exaggerated motion, hoping to relieve the pain. Behind his back, the paper in the wastebasket caught fire, and a brilliant blossom of flame shot toward the ceiling. Black smoke curled upward, darkening the white ceiling tiles. Then the conflagration threatened to ignite the paper on Maxwell's desk. Cursing furiously, the CIA man frantically ran out of the room and disappeared down the hallway.

"Dizzy son of a bitch, ain't he?" Roland commented.

Meanwhile Fetterman calmly reached over to the desk and grabbed the only Coke can with beads of moisture dripping down its sides. With one deliberate motion, he upended the contents on the fire, extinguishing it. "Yeah, ain't he?"

A flurry of footsteps clattered in the hallway, and they could hear someone breathing hard from exertion. A moment later Maxwell came running back into his office ready to do battle, fire extinguisher in hand. He skidded to a stop when he saw the soggy black mass in his wastebasket already turning cold.

Fetterman took careful aim, then flipped the empty Coke can into the trash. It clattered as it hit the rim, spun around once, then dropped out of sight. "What took you so long?" the master sergeant asked matter-of-factly.

Maxwell just stood there, realizing how stupid he looked. With perspiration beading his forehead, he struggled to catch his breath while he fidgeted with the fire extinguisher. Then, whirling around, he closed the door and returned to his desk.

"Your primary mission," he began, ignoring the previous excitement, "is to destroy a staging area west of Haiphong and perilously close to China." He smacked the wall map hard with an index finger, then traced a line from the Chinese border south to Son Tay. "The enemy is shipping war matériel by rail in from China into the staging area. From there, NVA regulars on their way south load the stuff on their backs and drag it down into our neck of the woods. We thought it might slow 'em down a bit if some of the AK-47s and ammo evaporated. And, hey, if some of their troops vaporize along with it, fine with me."

Gerber furrowed his brow. Although he couldn't pin down the specifics, something about Maxwell's presentation bothered him. Finally he asked, "How old is the intelligence data on Son Tay?"

"About a month old, maybe two," Maxwell said.

Gerber shook his head. "You want to drop us off deep behind enemy lines and you're asking me to risk the lives of me and my team members on stale intel? No way. We can't run this mission like that. The intel you've been providing us recently hasn't been reliable. By the time we infiltrate and get on-site, they could abandon that railhead and move it to a new location. Or they could double or even triple the garrison. It just doesn't make sense to waltz blindly into a situation like that."

Maxwell, ever the quintessential field operative, just grinned. He prided himself on being experienced in handling team commanders. All you had to do was sprinkle little bits of information in front of them, prod them into a corner, then watch them as they charged out with both fists raised. Usually they came up with the right idea on their own. This time would prove to be no exception. "You got any better ideas?" he asked nonchalantly.

"As a matter of fact, I do," Gerber said. "We'll infiltrate, lie low during the day and recon at night. If it looks like we have a reasonable chance of accomplishing our mission without getting our butts shot off, we'll do it. If not, we come home, and they'll never even know we were there."

Maxwell shrugged. "I can live with that."

"So can we," Gerber said, conscious of the irony of his statement.

"I've assigned two Kit Carson scouts to you for recon work," Maxwell continued. "They can move in close to the site without standing out. And since they're from the North to begin with, their dialects won't give them away if they're stopped and questioned by the local militia."

"Your ideas always sound good in theory," Gerber said, "but how do we know if these guys are reliable? Have they ever deployed with a spike team before? The last thing I want on my hands is a pair of double agents when I'm that far from home."

"An understandable concern," Maxwell muttered. "And, yes, these guys are solid, reliable assets. We've used them three times, and on each occasion they drew good reports from the team commanders, who, incidentally, all came back without a scratch and with their missions accomplished."

Without exchanging a word, the three Green Berets got out of their seats and turned toward the door. "You owe me a lighter," Fetterman said on the way out. "I'll collect from you when we get back."

When they had closed the door behind them, Maxwell frowned. "I sure hope you can, Tony. I sure as hell hope you can."

2

CONTINENTAL HOTEL
SAIGON

After the meeting with Jerry Maxwell at MACV Headquarters, Gerber ordered the team members to assemble in the lobby of the Continental Hotel at 6:00 p.m. sharp for what he jokingly referred to as their Last Supper. Fetterman took care of the logistics, reserving a separate room at the restaurant and ordering a sumptuous feast that included sirloin steaks, baked potatoes and sour cream. Dessert was a bottle of Beam's.

The rules to be observed during the Last Supper were simple: the SF troopers were to avoid talking about the upcoming behind-the-lines North Vietnam mission. Instead they were supposed to concentrate on war stories and women. No exceptions were to be tolerated.

Gerber pushed his plate away, the meal reduced to a few scraps of fat and a ravaged potato skin. Fetterman

and the others were still gabbing away and pushing
forkfuls of medium-rare into their mouths. Gerber
wondered if this was how it had been in England with
King Arthur and his round table. Then, like now, the
elite warriors were gathered to share a ritual meal before
a battle and regale each other with feats of bravery, real
and imagined. Only, instead of broadswords, Gerber's
foot soldiers carried M-16s and Ka-bar knives.

Sergeant Frank Umber was in the middle of a story.
"One night, oh, about 3:00 a.m., I had closed a guest-
house about twenty or so miles outside Bad Tolz and I
was driving back to the post when my headlights hit an
old man hitchhiking by the side of the road. He was an
old German who looked as if he'd been in a battle or
something. Blood was smeared across one side of his face
and the back of his hand. I remember his hand because
he was carrying a gym bag." Umber paused and took a
long pull on his beer.

Fetterman played the straight man. "Carrying a gym
bag, you say?"

"Yeah," Umber responded. "The same kind you
carried your jockstrap, gym shorts and tennis shoes to
school in. Anyway, the old guy got into my jeep and
wouldn't talk. Hell, I'm bighearted, but the main reason I'd given him a ride was so that he'd talk and help
keep me from falling asleep and running my jeep into a
tree. So I asked the old German what he had in the bag.

The German glared at me and said in perfect English, 'None of your fucking business.' The nerve of that guy. I give him a ride and he's rude. Pissed me off. I drove for a while, then got to wondering why he was so touchy and what he could possibly have in the bag. Maybe he was an old Nazi and was carrying around Adolf Hitler's head.''

''Or his dick,'' Roland cracked.

Umber grinned, then continued his story. ''So I asked the old German again, 'What's in the bag?' The old geezer glared at me and growled, 'None of your fucking business.' I'm telling you, the tone in his voice sent shivers up and down my spine. I kept my mouth shut after that. It didn't matter if he talked or not. By now my adrenaline was pumping. Then we got to the front gate of the post and I couldn't stand it anymore. I had to know what was in the bag. So I asked him what was in the bag one more time. He scowled at me, then mumbled, 'None of your fucking business.'

''That was it. I decided he and I were quits. I didn't care if it was cold out and snowing. So I pulled over to the side of the road and told him to get out. He didn't give me any trouble. He just opened the door, got out of the jeep and ran away, leaving his goddamn gym bag on the floor. I couldn't believe it.''

The room fell silent. After a while Roland couldn't stand it any longer. He had to know. "So what was in the bag?"

Umber looked him square in the eye, "None of your fucking business."

Moments later Fetterman nudged Roland. "I've got a theory about the Eighth," he murmured, his voice so quiet that only he and Roland could hear what was said.

"Theory? About what? What do you mean?"

"I'm willing to bet my stripes that there's a high incidence of freak accidents befalling the Eighth these days."

"I don't follow you," Roland said.

Fetterman grinned when he detected a slight wavering in Roland's response. He pressed on. "I bet a lot of the operational A-Detachments lose one, two or three guys every now and then, and that the chairborne rangers at HQ are never scratched. And don't tell me you don't know what I'm talking about. So tell me, how do they list the official cause of death—boating accidents, drownings . . . ?"

Roland didn't answer for a moment. When he started talking, his voice was solemn and unwavering. He spoke slowly and distinctly, carefully choosing his words. "Had a hometown buddy who joined the Air Force and became a U-2 pilot back in the early sixties. One day two officers knocked on his door at home and told his wife he'd been killed in a car wreck and that his body had been burned to ashes."

Fetterman nodded. "So that was the official version. What really happened?"

"He was hightailing it back from Russia toward his base in Izmir, Turkey. He nearly made it to the Black Sea when a MiG caught up with him and launched a rocket up his tailpipe. Joe never made it out of the cockpit. I hear his scorched flight helmet and part of his plane are in a museum in Moscow."

Fetterman scratched his chin. "So this sort of thing never happens in the Eighth, right?"

Roland nodded. "Yeah, thank God we never run clandestine missions into Latin America. We lose enough guys as it is. Surprising how many A-team members will go tarpon fishing at the mouth of the Chagres River, knowing those are shark-infested waters. There are so many sharks there that the Navy uses the immediate area for testing their shark repellent. Anyway, an SFer will be waist-deep in water and a bull shark will roll in on a wave and drag him down. Never find the body. Know what I mean?"

"Yeah," Fetterman said somberly. "That means an officer and a sergeant show up in on-base housing and knock on a door to tell the wife and kiddies that Daddy isn't coming home. He's been gone a week or two already, and he's never coming home."

The two men sat in silence. Fetterman's hunger had dissolved with their discussion. He picked up his remaining food with his fork, while Roland pushed his plate away and sipped some water.

To Fetterman, who had known nothing beyond the borders of Vietnam for what seemed like an eternity, the concept of any war that didn't involve NVA regulars and pajama-clad VC seemed unreal if not outright fantasy. The master sergeant cleared his throat. "Sergeant Roland," he said, "you ever do any tarpon fishing in the Canal Zone?"

Roland nodded. "Lots of times. Panama and other places here and there. Lost three buddies to the sharks. Three good men whose wives had to face an officer and a sergeant at their doorstep. Although, in some ways, I feel just as sorry for the messengers of death as for the bereaved."

Fetterman tugged at his ear. "When we were walking the halls at MACV HQ this afternoon, we talked about the CIB and how you don't have one."

"Yeah, so?"

Without saying another word, Fetterman unbuttoned his fatigue shirt, stuck a hand inside and removed the two clips that held his own Combat Infantryman's Badge in place. Then he handed the coveted award to Roland.

"What's this?" the staff sergeant asked.

"You've earned it," he said. "I've been to the O and I course at Fort Holabird and been knee-deep in spooks and sneaky pete logic. I know what you've probably been through. I suspect you know as much about this business as Gerber and me. I know the deal, Sergeant Roland. It may not be official. It may not be listed in your 201 file. The Department of Defense may not give you credit for the covert missions you've been running during your last tour. But I do."

Roland's eyes glowed like those of a little kid who had just been given a shiny new bike. "Well, thank you, Master Sergeant."

Without warning, Fetterman's eyebrows shot up. "Wait a minute," he said, grabbing the CIB. "Give me that." He pushed back his chair and trotted over to Gerber's side, leaving a befuddled Roland staring at his empty hand, where the CIB had been seconds before.

With the palm of his hand empty, but still warm from the feel of the CIB, Roland watched Fetterman and Gerber converse in an animated manner. Both were smiling when Fetterman banged his clenched fist on the tabletop, calling the room to order.

Gerber stood, then said, "Like knights at King Arthur's table, we're gathered here to honor one of our own. To honor courage and bravery. To honor deeds that can never be told publicly due to the interests of national security. Nevertheless, the Special Forces takes care of its own. With that in mind, Staff Sergeant Roland, please stand.''

Roland pushed back his chair and came to attention.

By now Fetterman had directed the waiter to fill all of the canteen cups with Beam's Choice, each cup now holding the rough equivalent of eight shots of whiskey.

Gerber continued with his speech. ''We'll now raise our glasses to toast a brave warrior. Strike that. A brave fisherman. A brave fisherman who has vanquished many Communist tarpon from the waters of Central and South America at great risk to himself. To him we toast.''

Gerber took a long pull from his canteen cup, and the other members of the team followed suit.

Fetterman took the floor. ''And to further commemorate these long-unrecognized deeds of bravery, we award to this brave warrior/fisherman the Combat Fisherman's Badge of Courage.''

Holding the CIB in his hand, Fetterman approached Roland. Standing face-to-face with him, he slammed the exposed CIB pins against Roland's chest. The sharp metal pierced Roland's flesh, and the badge stuck like glue.

Gerber set his cup of whiskey down on the plywood table stared directly at Roland and saluted. Fetterman and the others followed suit. Then Gerber cried out, ''For these nameless deeds in nameless rivers and streams, we salute you, Sergeant Roland.''

The others chimed in unison, "We salute you, Sergeant Roland."

Then Fetterman yanked the CIB off Roland's chest. "What the . . . ?" the staff sergeant cried.

Fetterman grinned at him.

Gerber coughed, then said, "Because these brave deeds revolve around the classified activities of certain intelligence agencies and an elite military organization that shall remain forever nameless, the award to you today of the Combat Fisherman's Badge of Courage is classified. You may never acknowledge its award to you or that this ceremony ever took place. You were never here. We were never here. The medal was never here." Gerber sat down. "Now, what were we talking about?" he asked with a deadpan expression.

Roland understood. Smirking, he sat down and took a long pull of whiskey, enjoying the burn all the way down his throat until it imploded in his stomach. He felt good. Even if the paperwork didn't reflect his accomplishments, the men he felt kinship with did. That was important to him. That and the fact that he'd be going on the mission as an equal and not an untried commodity. Roland felt very good indeed.

3

ISOLATION COMPOUND SOMEWHERE IN SOUTH VIETNAM

The isolation compound reminded Roland of the one back in Panama at Fort Randolph, where he had spent so many days and nights preparing for direct-action missions. Like those at Fort Randolph, this post's high stone walls were ringed with coils of concertina wire. There was only way way in or out—a single gate guarded by sandbagged emplacements featuring 30-caliber tripod-mounted machine guns manned by ill-tempered itchy-fingered MPs. No unauthorized personnel were allowed in or out. Inside the compound there was a large clearing occupied by a single building housing a dozen two-man rooms and a conference center.

Gerber, Fetterman, Roland and Umber sat on gray metal folding chairs at the front of the briefing room, steaming mugs of coffee in their hands.

Roland reflected on how, save for the air-conditioning, the conference room could have been located anywhere the Special Forces had an installation: Fort Bragg, Bad Tolz, Oklahoma, Panama, Nha Trang. It didn't seem to matter. It was as if all briefing rooms came out of the same mold. The walls were always adorned with the same U.S. government printing office lithographs: artists impressions of famous and not-so-famous U.S. Army victories. And, as usual, at the front of the room there was a wooden podium, an easel for charts, a pull-down movie screen and a long briefing table for SR-71 photos and intel reports. Behind the table, hanging on the wall, were a pair of AK-47s with their bayonets extended. Below the brace of weapons were a pair of bullet-riddled, bloodstained black pajamas and a placard proclaiming the deceased Vietcong as a hero of Khe Sanh who had gloriously given his life so that Americans might live.

Most of the room was taken up by several rows of gray metal folding chairs. But on this day the room was empty except for Gerber and his men, who had gathered together in the conference center to receive a more specialized briefing from Maxwell. The CIA man stood at the table, sifting through the dozens of necessary SR-71 photos.

Gerber shifted impatiently in his chair. Notepad in one hand and a ballpoint pen in the other, he was anxious to get on with the briefing and the logistics of the mission.

Finally Maxwell was ready. "This is your target," he told them, nodding at the enlisted man in the back of the room. A moment later the lights went out and the slide projector blinked on, bathing the dark room in a hazy blue light.

Maxwell's voice pierced the darkness, its echo resounding off the walls of the nearly empty room. "As you learned at MACV HQ the other morning, your area of operations will be Son Tay in the North." Suddenly the movie screen was filled with the image of a railway staging area. Roland recognized the reconnaissance photo as the kind taken by a high-altitude SR-71, the famous Blackbird spy plane that flew at more than eighty thousand feet and at such high speed that it could outrun rockets and bullets. The aircraft flew so fast that no Blackbird had ever been knocked out of the sky.

The series of photos showed incredible detail. Beyond the ability to count the number of railroad cars, buildings and petroleum tanks, the photographic resolution was so good that they were able to spot individual enemy soldiers walking their posts. If they had wanted to, they could have even picked out the railroad ties in the track bed.

For over an hour Maxwell called slides up onto the screen and provided a running commentary on the significance of the images to Gerber's mission. Finally he called out to the projectionist, "Hit the switch, will you, Private?" The overhead fluorescent lights lit up the room, and Gerber blinked for a moment, giving his eyes a chance to adjust to the brightness.

By now Maxwell had left the podium and was stationed at the long gray metal table where he unfolded the first in a series of maps and spread it out. Gerber noticed how the Yuan River valley cut through their area of operations. The Yuan, called the Song Hong Ka by the Vietnamese, was an inland waterway that coursed out of the south Chinese province of Yunnan and curved in a southeasterly direction through North Vietnam's rice paddies and rain forest. Then the Yuan made a radical bend southward, dipped and curved near Son Tay and finally straightened and flowed on through the center of downtown Hanoi to the delta and on out to the Gulf of Tonkin and the South China Sea.

Maxwell reminded them of how the military equipment was coming out of China on a railroad that paralleled the Yuan from the Chinese border to the place where the river made a radical bend to the south at Son Tay. "And, of course, that's your mission—to vaporize the staging area there as well as any enemy troops that get in the way."

Gerber and his men studied the map. Superimposed on the blues, greens and browns were a maze of looping ridge lines that indicated the jungle-covered mountains and flooded rice paddies. They could also plainly see the highways, roads and, most importantly, the railroad Maxwell was talking about.

The CIA man swept his hand across the map. Again, as he had done with the photos, he pointed out pertinent information and provided commentary. Everyone in the spike team listened intently, since they wouldn't be allowed to infiltrate with maps or any other references and would have to memorize all of the details of their mission, things such as radio call signs, primary and secondary frequencies, grid coordinates, assembly and extraction points and so on.

With all of that in mind, Gerber's team studied how the double row of railroad tracks came down from the north, then began a long, slow curve eastward in the general direction of Hanoi and Haiphong harbor. Individual close-ups of the staging area proper showed them that at the beginning of the curve and on the north side of the tracks there was a series of sidings packed with boxcars, which the experts calculated were loaded with small arms and tens of thousands of rounds of ammunition, hand grenades and RPG-2 rounds.

Maxwell opened his aluminum briefcase and brought out a stack of eight-by-ten glossy photos that represented a sampling of the slides they had already looked at. Gerber leafed through them with Fetterman at his side and Roland and Umber looking over their shoulders.

The CIA man provided the commentary. "Most of the freight that passes through Son Tay is small-arms ammunition and weapons, although some of their demolition supplies are known to filter through, as well. This rolling ammo dump is your primary target."

Gerber held up a grainy close-up of the tank farm adjacent to the railyard. Fetterman counted three rows of five tanks. Comparing their relative size to the railroad cars and buildings, there was no question that they were huge.

Maxwell pointed at the photo. "Here's where they store diesel fuel for the locomotives and probably gasoline for their motor pool, too. We estimate a combined capacity totaling over one million barrels. That's your secondary target."

Roland whistled, then exclaimed, "Whoosh. Kaboom."

Gerber nodded imperceptibly at Fetterman, then looked directly at Maxwell. Fetterman started to grin. "Can you go back to that overview, the far shot that shows the topographical relationship of everything? And I'd like to see it blown up."

"Certainly," Maxwell said, motioning to the private running the projector. The room lights winked out and the eerie blue projector light blinked on. After a few false starts, the slide Fetterman requested was back up on the screen.

"What have you noticed, Tony?" Maxwell asked in a carefully measured voice. "I figure if anyone could spot what's wrong with this picture, it's you." There was a strange smile on his face.

"Proximity," Fetterman answered.

Gerber snapped his fingers, then piped in, "Exactly. The tank farm looks like it's uphill from the siding where they park all the boxcars full of ammo."

"You're absolutely right," Maxwell said. "Our agent in place tells us security is fairly tight in the railyard. Roving guards work their way through every half hour, but there's zero coverage on the side of the hill where the fuel dump is."

Fetterman seemed amused. "So we set shaped charges at the base of the tanks, punch a few holes in their sides and the diesel fuel flows downhill and pools around the boxcars. Then we fire off some tracer rounds, duck and hope we don't get incinerated, too."

"Exactly," Maxwell answered. "The boxcars explode, the fuel dump burns like nobody's business and then you guys hustle on home."

Fetterman's smile faded. He was beginning to get a handle on the intricacies of the mission that had been presented to them. He shook his head. "No. There's something radically wrong. You're not tell us something important. There's some critical element you've neglected to tell us. It can't be this easy. It never is and never will be."

Gerber nodded. "I agree with Tony. Seems to me an operation like this would be more adequately performed by a B-52 raid. In fact, a single B-52 could wipe the installation off the face of the earth. Nice, clean and sterile. Why bother sending us in? It doesn't make sense. Things can go wrong in a hurry on the ground. We could get killed before we even get in the place. On the other hand, the only way the B-52 guys could fuck up is by missing the target."

Maxwell's face reddened. He stood at the front of the room, twirling his pointer between his fingers. After a moment, he sent the projectionist out of the room. Then he addressed Gerber's team. "The official reason for sending you in and not calling in an air strike is that President Johnson has limited the scope of bombing raids, and Son Tay is beyond the allowable perimeter. It's frustrating as hell, believe me. Here we have a nice big fat target of opportunity and it's just out of range by ten klicks. Ten fucking klicks. We begged the Pentagon, but they wouldn't budge off their fat asses. So all I can say is sorry. As much as we'd like, we can't bend the rules on this one. A direct-action ground mission is okay, but no air strike.''

"I see.'' Gerber said. "So if that's the official position, allow us the simple luxury of a reality check. Since we're the ones risking our lives to avoid political embarrassment, what's the real reason for this mission?''

Maxwell took a deep breath, then exhaled. "You know me pretty well, so I won't insult your intelligence by lying. But I can't tell you the truth, either. So I won't say anything at all. That is, other than to tell you something you never heard from me: stay on your toes at Son Tay. Keep in mind things aren't always what they seem to be, if you know what I mean.''

The room was silent. The only sound was the tireless whirring of the clock on the wall as its second hand ticked off a full minute.

Maxwell walked to the door and called the projectionist into the room to run some more slides. Then he turned and said, "We've got some other problems to work out, so we might as well get on with it. First up is insertion.''

Roland grumbled. "Sounds like we're going to get the usual insertion on this mission, if you catch my drift.''

Maxwell ignored the crack and continued with the briefing. "Insertion into this location is a particularly hairy problem. Obviously a HALO jump out of a B-52 is the preferred method, but this close to China the higher-ups are afraid a B-52 on Chinese radar would attract considerable interest and therefore too much attention to your mission."

"So what are you recommending? That we walk in from Laos?" Gerber asked sarcastically.

"Well, no, of course not. It seems to me a healthy alternative would be to fly in from the southwest from one of the dirt airstrips in Laos. Make a low-altitude, low-opening jump from a C-123. Say at five hundred feet."

"There are certain benefits to that scenario," Roland suggested. "Relatively short flight time and low fatigue factor for the jumpers. Also, we could fly undetected under their radar. Oh, and most important of all, if the rigger fucks up any of the parachutes, we'll die in great agony before we have a chance to pop our reserve canopies."

"If we want to infiltrate the area of operations undetected, we've got little choice other than some variant of LALO," Gerber added.

Fetterman agreed. "No matter how you look at it, infiltrating deep behind enemy lines presents inherent risks. There are no guarantees. This is just one of the dangers that goes with the job."

"Then I'll coordinate the air transport for you," Maxwell said. "And I'll give you the rest of the day to work out your plan of attack once you're on the ground.

Let me know what webgear and weapons you want. I'll arrange all the logistical details. You know the drill. You've done this dozens of times before.''

The meeting broke up, and Maxwell hustled out of the room. Silently the team pulled their chairs up to the long table and waited for the projectionist to leave. Once he had closed the door behind him, the team began their strategy session.

With the topographical map spread across the table-top, the men leaned over and studied it intently. Blue, green and brown lines described in intricate detail every ridge line, rice paddy, mountaintop and forest. Gerber pointed to a spot on the map and turned to Fetterman. ''Tony, how about we use this road here as a drop zone? That locates us within ten klicks of the railroad depot, but far enough away from it so that they won't pay much attention to the C-123. In fact, they may not even hear it. The ten klicks shouldn't take us more than a couple of hours to hump.''

Fetterman studied the map, contemplating all the possibilities. Finally he said, ''Yeah. I think that might work. I've jumped better DZs and I've jumped worse. Most of it's luck, anyway.''

''So that's settled.'' Gerber said. ''Now we need to decide how we're getting into the depot. And like I said yesterday in Maxwell's office, I don't trust his intel. Let's plan on doing our own intel before we go making any mad dashes into a heavily armed installation.'' Gerber grinned at Fetterman. ''I wouldn't want to get you killed and piss off Ma Fetterman. She'd never forgive me. Besides, it would blow my shot at the Nobel peace prize this year.''

Fetterman grinned back. ''Ma thanks you, sir.''

''What about gear?'' Gerber asked. ''AKs seems to be the weapon of choice for this operation.''

''Roger that,'' Fetterman agreed. ''If they hear AK fire, they'll likely figure it's their own troops jacking around. A burst from an M-16 would be a dead giveaway for sure.''

Roland asked to be assigned to weapons. ''I want to make sure they're all milled receivers. We should specify Russian manufacture only. No Chinese junk. I've had bad luck with the stamped variety. Also we'll want Czech or Soviet headstamped ammo. It's more reliable, with less misfiring.''

''You've got it,'' Fetterman said, pleased that Roland had involved himself with the nuts and bolts of the mission without prompting, and also that the staff sergeant seemed to know weapons. With him along, perhaps the mission would end up working out after all.

4

ISOLATION COMPOUND
SOMEWHERE IN SOUTH
VIETNAM

"Many thanks to our friends the Israelis for providing us with the necessary implements of battle," Umber chortled as he picked up a brand-new AK-47. "They probably captured this cache of weapons during the Six Day War, kicking ass and taking names."

"You make it sound like a long time ago," Roland said. "It was just last year."

"Hey, I was there, sort of," Umber said. "The Tenth spent three days on alert, twenty yards away from a C-130, linking M-60 rounds in case we got the orders to deploy."

"Where was this?" Roland asked.

"Tenth Group, Bad Tolz. I was on an A-team. The ammo went but we stayed."

Roland nodded. "I hear that's good duty if you speak German and like to drink *beaucoup* beer."

Umber feigned great despair. "Yeah, but the Tenth is moving to Fort Devens next year. No more blue-eyed blond fräuleins, guesthouses and German beer."

Roland grabbed one of the AKs and pushed a cleaning rod and patch down the muzzle. A moment later greasy red Cosmoline squirted out of the receiver like toothpaste out of a tube. The two Special Forces sergeants cleaned each of the weapons in turn, scraping off the big clumps of grease, then following up with rags soaked in lacquer thinner to wash off the remaining film.

"We bringing handguns on this mission?" Umber asked.

"Nope," Roland replied.

"Why not? I feel naked without one."

"Weight. Every pound counts. Only time you need a handgun is for close fighting. We get into that tight a squeeze and we're fucked. We don't need handguns on this trip."

"If we did get to carry one, what kind would you bring?"

"Me, I'm a revolver man," Roland said as he put down one AK-47 and started to unwrap another in preparation for removing its protective coating of Cosmoline.

"A revolver," Umber exclaimed incredulously. "You mean, like an Old West six-shooter? No way. I like a fast-shooting automatic, say the Browning Hi-Power."

Roland suppressed a thin smile. "Not for me, man. It's revolvers all the way, as far as I'm concerned. With a double-action Smith or Colt, you just get it out of the holster and squeeze the trigger."

"So why not just carry the government model 1911A1?" Umber countered.

Roland shook his head. "Nope. With a revolver you don't have to pump the slide to get a shell into the chamber. Even a fool knows it's not safe to carry a .45 automatic with a round in the chamber and the safety off. I saw a guy in Guatemala, one of their rich boy captains, carrying a pearl-handled 1911 in a tooled leather holster. He was playing wild, wild West, accidentally knocked off the safety and blew his own leg to bits. Nearly bled to death. With a revolver all you've got to do is pull back the hammer and fire." Beginning to sweat, Roland peeled off his shirt and began to rub his shoulder, massaging the muscles as if they were stiff or painful.

Umber paused to watch. Directly below Roland's left shoulder was a quarter-sized indentation. "How did you get that? Was it a bullet or shrapnel?"

Roland shook his head and continued kneading his muscles. "Neither one. Took a direct hit from a Supersonic bird."

Umber looked puzzled. "Huh?"

Roland grinned. He had Umber right where he wanted him, so he immediately launched into a story he had told so many times that it was as polished as a brigadier general's silver stars.

"A couple of years ago I was riding my Harley-Davidson down in Panama on the Pan-American Highway. I was going fifty miles an hour when I smacked into a long-beaked bird. You should have seen the feathers fly." He paused just long enough to thump the spot on his chest for effect, then continued with his tale. "The bird knocked me clean off my bike. The Harley went off the road and smacked into a tree, while I went tumbling down the road, head over heals. Good thing I was wearing a full set of leathers and a helmet."

Umber snorted. "Were you hurt?"

"Damn near killed, hoss. I got up and brushed myself off. You should have seen me. I looked like I'd been in a fight with a lion. My helmet was shattered as if somebody had whacked it with a sledgehammer."

A moody look stole into Umber's eyes as he studied Roland's scar.

After several minutes, Roland asked, "What's on your mind, hoss? You thinking about your wife again?"

Umber shook his head. "No; not that. I've been thinking about the other night at the restaurant. I heard you and Fetterman talking about tarpon fishing."

"And?"

"And I think I understand."

"Oh," Roland murmured.

Umber pointed at the wound. "I'm willing to bet a lot of guys in the Eighth have had motorcycle accidents like yours. You know, run into birds on the road. Accidents like that happen all the time when you go tarpon fishing, right?"

Roland grinned. "You're a smart guy, Umber. You'll work out fine in the North."

LATER THAT NIGHT the team members sequestered themselves in two-man rooms. The lights winked out, and the men lay on their bunks, covered by poncho liners to warm them against the frigid air-conditioning.

"Hey, Roland, you asleep?" Umber called out.

"Yeah," came the good-natured reply. "What do you want?"

"Do you understand women?"

Roland sat up in bed. "Son, nobody understands women. Not old men, women themselves, psychiatrists, beauty shop operators, gynecologists, rabbis, priests, plumbers, electricians, nobody. Why do you ask?"

"Well, I was just wondering."

"You get another letter from your wife?"

"Yeah." Umber muttered.

Roland detected a certain glumness in his partner's voice. The guy had a problem. He considered Umber bright enough, but somehow the guy had linked up with a bad lady. Umber had shown Roland some of the letters from his wife. It didn't look good for the guy. Roland suspected the woman had married him, knowing he was going to Vietnam and would likely get killed since he was in the Special Forces. If that happened, she'd be the beneficiary of a ten-thousand-dollar life insurance policy. On the other hand, if Umber came back, she'd be sitting pretty, having drawn a monthly allotment all along. She could just divorce the poor slob if she wanted to. Roland shook his head. He'd seen the scenario over and over again.

"It's like this, Umber," he finally said. "There's two kinds of women in the world. One kind is like steel, and that's the kind you've got to avoid at all costs. The other kind is like silk. And if I need to explain any more to you than that, then you're a lost cause, so fuck you."

"I've got to disagree with you. My wife, Crystal, is part steel and part silk. I guess that's what makes her so interesting to me."

"King cobras are interesting, too. That doesn't mean a guy wants to nest with a snake to check it out. You've shown me those letters your wife sent you. I don't think you're paranoid. I think she's mind-fucking you on purpose. Some women are into that."

"I'm just worried," Umber said.

"Yeah, I can tell. But we've got to keep our minds on the mission. You need to put her out of your head until we get back, or your daydreaming may get both of us killed. Fair enough?"

"Yeah, sure," Umber mumbled unconvincingly.

Roland rolled over and soon fell sound asleep. At first he dreamed about the women he'd met in the bordellos of Panama, the beautifully built Colombian women who'd set his heart aflutter. But by the middle of the night, his dreams entered virgin territory. Even though he had never even seen a snapshot of her, Roland saw Umber's wife—a beautiful, big-breasted woman with deep blue eyes. The kind of woman who caused most men to tremble when she smiled. In his dream Umber's wife walked directly to Roland's side and squeezed into a booth next to him.

So that was it, thought Roland. He was in a bar somewhere. He didn't recognize the strange place because it was too hazy with cigarette smoke and the glare of neon lights that turned everything alternately red and blue. When Umber's wife, Crystal, smiled at him seductively, he wasn't affected. He'd learned long ago that he was better off having nothing to do with a woman like her. She spelled deep trouble, the kind that was hard to shake.

After a few minutes of eye contact and rubbing her hand up and down Roland's thigh, Crystal lost interest and walked off, leaving him along with his rum and Coke. Roland breathed a deep sigh of relief, took a long pull on his drink, the swung around and surveyed the crowd.

After a few moments he saw Maureen, his own wife, and Crystal talking with each other, laughing and giggling as if they were old friends. How could that be, though? Roland's heart started pounding. He could feel the anxiety welling up inside of him. What could they possibly have in common? he wondered.

He watched in horror as they walked over to a table of men with long hair. Hippies. One of the men was wearing a peace medallion around his neck.

Maureen and Crystal sat down with the hippies, and someone handed them a beer. Maureen took a sip, then laughed at something one of the hippies said.

Roland's blood started heating up. He tried to slide out of the booth and head over to his wife, with the intention of making her come home with him. But something glued him in place. His arms wouldn't move and his legs were frozen. He just sat there, powerless, as one of the hippies put an arm around Maureen's shoulder, then kissed her. Maureen seemed to enjoy it.

"No, no!" Roland yelled. His own screams woke him up. Sitting bolt upright in bed, the poncho liner clutched tightly in his arms, he tried to breathe properly as his heart slammed against his chest. He was shaking. The vision was still vivid in his memory. He could see his wife nestled in the hippie's arms. And even though he knew it had only been a dream, the image still bothered him intensely. Everything had seemed so real. Where had the dream come from? His wife was dead, so why was he worried about her faithfulness? It didn't make sense.

Roland forced himself to lie down again. Still troubled by the strange dream, he just lay on the bed, unable to sleep. Finally he decided to think about the mission and wait for dawn. Some Green Beret, he told himself. He'd warned Umber to get his mind off Crystal, and here he was thinking about Umber's wife *and* his own dead Maureen. Roland prayed dawn would come fast.

5

FLIGHT LINE VANG PAO, LAOS

Gerber and his men pored over their maps for the last time and quizzed one another on grid coordinates, primary and secondary assembly points, radio call signs and frequencies. They checked, then double-checked the radio transceivers, plastic explosives, electric detonators, AK-47s, grenades and rucksacks.

Garbed in camouflage jungle fatigues, Gerber stood in the middle of the group of men, clipboard in hand, checking off the inventory. "AK-47 ammo, 7.62 mm," he called out, his voice filling the giant airplane hangar.

As he studied the inventory, Gerber's steel-blue eyes reflected quiet resolution. But when he was out in the field, the same eyes smoldered with grim determination. Now, as he bent over the inventory sheets, he slid a hand grenade out of its black protective shipping tube, then held the explosive in the palm of his hand. He studied its squat green body. He liked the cold feel of the one-pound hunk of high explosive that once detonated would scatter countless white-hot steel fragments in every direction. Staring at the M-26 hand grenade, he found himself wondering how he'd come to be in the company of men who only felt at home amid the heat of battle.

Gerber was a career soldier through and through, the kind of man who liked the sound of helicopter gunships beating the air overhead, accompanied by the crackle of small-arms fire stinging his ears and incoming mortar rounds bouncing around in the mud. Being close to death made Gerber feel very much alive. Running direct-action missions into North Vietnam was what Gerber was all about.

He glanced up from his reverie just in time to see Jerry Maxwell walk toward him. The CIA agent held out a hand and smiled. "Just stopped by to wish you guys luck."

"Good or bad?" Gerber snapped.

"Good, of course," Maxwell replied. "You ready to knock off your target and be home in time for a traditional Fourth of July feast of hot dogs and potato salad? Of course, I've heard through the grapevine that this year there may be a pig roast to supplement the hot dogs.

Either way I'll personally make sure they save you a mug of beer and a full plate at the embassy bash in Saigon.''

Gerber imagined himself on the embassy grounds, just back from the mission, sweaty and smelly with blood-soiled jungle fatigues and a week's growth of beard, while the embassy types in starched shirts and tropical-weight white suits stared at him as if he were the Creature from the Black Lagoon. The Special Forces captain allowed himself the luxury of a few moments of wry speculation, imagining a fine-boned embassy woman from New England attempting to make polite conversation with Fetterman. But the image was too ludicrous to entertain for very long.

Instead, he slipped back into reality as he and Maxwell stood silently in the hangar, watching Fetterman and the other members of the team dividing two-and-a-half-pound blocks of C-4 among the rucksacks. The smell of formaldehyde from the plastic explosives was thick in the air. When he had been a junior officer fresh out of OCS and a rookie in the Special Forces, the pungent odor had offended him. But he had grown truly fond of the plastic explosives after its use had saved his life a number of times.

Gerber didn't say anything for at least five minutes. Finally Maxwell broke the silence. ''Why do you still go on these covert missions, Mack? You could always get a desk job at S-2 back in Nha Trang. You're not getting any younger. I bet at night in the jungle the cold seeps clear through to your bones. And it probably takes five or ten minutes every morning to shake it free.''

Gerber looked at Maxwell as if he were crazy. ''Quit the Special Forces? Have you been drinking, Jerry?''

Maxwell shrugged. ''You wouldn't have to resign from the SF. I'm just saying a desk job would be safer.''

Gerber scowled. ''The day I quit the Special Forces will be the day you tell the truth for the first time.''

Maxwell blinked but didn't say anything.

''Do you really want to know why I do what I do?''

Maxwell nodded.

''Because I happen to like it. Sitting behind a desk would be the end of the world for me. I'm not cut out to be a paper pusher. I'd turn to fat and spend all my time being irritable. I'd become just like you Maxwell. And my pride would never allow me to sink that low.''

Maxwell absentmindedly stroked a finger along the pink-tinged scar that slashed across his throat, the result of an attempt to cut his throat in a Saigon alley one night. ''Christ, what could you possibly like about this dirty business? People die horrible deaths in strange lands. Most of the time the bodies are never even given a decent burial. Obviously you like it or you wouldn't be here. But why do you like it? That's what I'd want to know—why?''

Gerber shrugged. "Simple. Fear's a better high than any drug known to man. The adrenaline pumping in my veins keeps me young."

Maxwell grunted. "Yeah, well, death is the end of all fear, Mack. I'd rather get old than take unnecessary chances."

Gerber grinned and deliberately pulled the pin on the grenade he was still holding. Pressing the arm lever flat against the side of the grenade, he slapped the explosive device into Maxwell's hand, curling the CIA man's fingers around the safety lever. Then he smiled and dangled the pin in front of Maxwell.

"Goddamn it, Mack, what the hell are you doing?" Scowling, he grabbed the pin out of Gerber's hand and tried to slip it back into the grenade without letting the lever fly up. When he succeeded, he tossed the grenade back into Gerber's hands, telling him, "By the way, there's been a little change in plans."

Gerber furrowed his eyebrows. "Maybe you'd better think twice, Jerry. Fetterman and I usual murder bearers of bad news on the eve of a mission."

"Your assets, the Kit Carson's scouts, have been unavoidably delayed. They're still up north, stuck in the AO. You'll link up with them on the DZ. That's the bad news. Good news is they're going to function as pathfinders for you. You'll make good time from the DZ to the target without any screwing around."

"Unavoidably delayed?" Gerber said wryly. "I don't like the sound of that. Maybe you'd better define your terms."

Eavesdropping on the conversation, Fetterman set down two blocks of C-4 and walked over to join Gerber. "Let me guess," he said. "Something went wrong."

"Sort of," Maxwell said, looking down at his feet, then glancing at Fetterman and smiling.

"Sort of," Gerber intoned. "You'd better explain yourself fast, Jerry. Real fast."

Fetterman answered for Maxwell, "It means somebody got killed. Sort of. Am I right, Maxwell?"

The CIA man nodded. "We're not sure of the details yet, but the two American officers who were with the Kit Carson scouts are presumed KIAs. When we find out more details, we'll encrypt it and send it over the radio to you on one of your regularly scheduled communications."

"Like I said in your office, Maxwell," Gerber growled, "your intel and your personnel haven't been very reliable lately, have they? You told me these scouts were reliable. But this situation is beginning to stink already."

Maxwell didn't answer. Instead, he turned and walked away.

"Do you think maybe we ought to consider scrubbing the mission?" Fetterman asked Gerber. "Seems to me it's already compromised, and there's no sense getting ourselves killed.''

Gerber swore. ''I don't know, Tony. We're under orders. We'll just be extra careful once we're on the ground.''

Gerber motioned to the pilot, who was already running a preflight checklist inside the cockpit. A moment later the port engine's yellow-tipped propeller began to spin. Then the radial engine sputtered, pushing out a black column of oily smoke.

With both engines warming up, Gerber and his men trooped aboard the aircraft, lugging rucksacks and rifles. Once inside, they eased back into the troop seats, pulled the wide seat belts across their laps and latched them. Sitting on the ground with the ramp down and the doors open, the heat and humidity were insufferable, and the men were soon soaked in sweat. While they were getting settled, the crew chief went from man to man, handing out disposable earplugs from a big jar. Fetterman refused the offer as he stuffed a .45-caliber bullet into each ear. ''Works just as well!'' he shouted above the roar of the engines.

Finally the Air America pilot taxied to the edge of the runway, where he locked the brakes and throttled the engines to takeoff rpm. The tips of the props blurred. Both engines at full bore, the airframe rattled, kicking up clouds of dust at Gerber's feet.

With the brakes released, the plane accelerated down the runway, its tires clicking as they crossed the cracks in the concrete. When he was going fast enough, the pilot eased back the yoke and climbed away from the Laotian soil. At a thousand feet he leveled off and pointed the nose of the plane in the direction of the Yuan River valley.

ON THE GROUND at Drop Zone Fauber two men hunkered down in a field of shoulder-high grass, waiting to mark the drop zone for Gerber. They had already laid out a dozen coffee cans full of gasoline and weighted down with handfuls of sand.

Their instructions were simple: when the plane came from the west, they were to torch the gasoline. From the air, Gerber and the pilot would spot the flames and see the drop zone.

The pathfinders had picked a valley with jungle on three sides and a mountain on the other. From their training with the Green Berets at Nha Trang, they knew paratroopers liked long, grassy fields without any rocks that might break leg or ankle bones. This spot was a good drop zone; the only hazard was the slippery oxen dung scattered everywhere.

The two men talked to pass the time. The thin one, who bore a mustache, grinned broadly. He had been telling his partner about his cultural experiences in Saigon. "So, after I paid her the money, she took off her dress and asked me to—"

"Ssh! Listen!" his friend interrupted.

Both men turned to face the sky. They could hear a distant rumbling. Ears cocked, they listened intently as the droning got louder.

"Shall we light the markers?" the one with the mustache asked.

"Yes. Give me the matches."

They struck matchsticks on their wooden-stocked SKS rifles and lit the beacons one by one. Soon the Americans would be there to meet them.

THE PILOT FLEW as low as he dared, barely skimming over the treetops. The C-123 dipped into valleys and climbed over the hills.

Gerber knew the roller-coaster procedure was extremely dangerous. Once, when they'd been deep in North Vietnam on a mission, they'd encountered a C-123 that had broadsided a tree. It hadn't been a pretty sight.

Gerber stared out of the aircraft porthole and watched the engine expel blue exhaust flames. Inside the cabin the air was thick and moist. Gerber could feel the sweat flow down his back.

Suddenly Roland asked, "What altitude did you say we're jumping from?"

"Five hundred feet," Gerber said.

"I hate parachutes."

Gerber knew what was on Roland's mind. There was no reserve chute. Since they were jumping so close to the ground, if the main canopy failed, there wouldn't be enough time for a reserve to deploy, which meant there was no need to wear one.

Gerber drummed his fingers on the stock of his AK-47. The airplane engines droned on and on. He was tired of waiting. This was the part of a mission he hated most. Boredom, anticipation, inaction killed him more than danger. Unlike Roland, he looked forward to parachuting. He smiled grimly. Soon he would have all the action he wanted.

6

INN OF ETERNAL SOLITUDE NEAR SON TAY, NORTH VIETNAM

The Inn of Eternal Solitude was a back-country tavern with a handful of rooms surrounding the dance floor. In ancient times the rooms were reserved for weary travelers, but since World War II they housed the local militia, and a handful of working girls, even though such a practice was officially frowned on by the communist Party. At night beer flowed like water. And twinkling red and blue light bulbs strung around the rafters barely lit the great hall while soldiers and rice farmers rubbed elbows and got drunk.

Just a short walk up the trail from the garrison outside the staging area at Son Tay's railyard, off-duty soldiers began to wander in with the fading light. The tables and chairs quickly filled with hard-drinking men who sauntered in and stacked their rifles before bellying up to the bar for a drink.

Eventually a short man who barely weighed a hundred pounds sauntered in. He was dressed in a khaki uniform with a red patch and star on the collar. On his head he wore an officer's sun helmet marked with a red star. Some of his friends had preceded him and now sat at a table tucked into one corner.

"Hey, Tran, come join us." one of the called out.

"Have a drink," a second insisted.

Tran came over and sat down with them. One of the men poured him a drink and shoved it in front of him. Tran and his friends gulped down beer after beer and swapped lies until Tran noticed two Russian military advisers strutting up to the bar. Both were escorted by Vietnamese women from the village.

One of the Russian advisers, a tall blond man, held up four fingers and called out to the bartender in Vietnamese, "Four vodkas, comrade. We want to get your women drunk and then take advantage of them." The adviser leered at the bartender as he fondled the woman by his side.

Tran spit angrily on the floor. "Russian pigs. I wish they'd stay away from our women." He heard the women's laughter and cursed silently. "One of these days," he grumbled, "I'll kill one of them." Then he rested his hand on the butt of the automatic pistol hidden under his shirt. "I'll kill one," he muttered, "just to see what it feels like."

Minutes later Tran excused himself and walked back to the barracks. He often bragged to his comrades about how his night vision was as keen as a jungle cat's. He never tripped on rocks or stumbled in the ruts that fissured the road. Now, as he picked his way through the night air, he heard the cries of howler monkeys somewhere off in the jungle.

Tran was a country boy and knew the sounds of the jungle well. Only since he had joined the People's Army had he been required to wallow in the filth and stink of the city—the stagnant puddles of water in alleys and trash thrown out of windows onto the streets. He prayed to Buddha that the war would soon be won, that the Americans would go home and that he could spend his days hunting animals, not men. At the moment, though, all of that was impossible.

Tran shuddered when he recalled the only battle he had ever been in, a mass assault on a Special Forces border camp. In the middle of all the shooting and the shrieks of the dead and dying, he had turned and run. His entire platoon had been wiped out, and Tran was the only survivor. Luckily none of his comrades had lived to report his cowardice. In fact, due to an ironic twist of fate, and Communist propaganda, he had been decorated for bravery. But Tran knew the truth, as did the ghosts of his fallen comrades, who still taunted him mercilessly in nightmares.

Tran wondered if the Americans told war stories. He chuckled to himself as he imagined supposedly brave heroes bragging about being the only survivor of a platoon. How easy that would be when only you knew the truth and all the others were dead.

But that single incident of cowardice had changed Tran's life forever. He had vowed never again to allow fear to influence his actions. His resolve, coupled with the shame he felt over the death of his comrades, worked magnificently. Bicycle Chain Tran had earned his nickname in South Vietnam, where his specialty was working at night. Alone, cloaked in darkness, he prowled around American perimeters, armed with nothing more than a simple bicycle chain.

Tran's eyes glimmered at the remembrance of his accomplishments. He would sneak up behind an unwary American GI, who was drunk or too tired to pay attention to his surroundings, whirl the bicycle chain overhead and then smack it like a bullwhip against the back of the enemy's head. Tran smiled, relishing the thunk the chain made when it cracked a skull, how it shattered bone and unleashed a torrent of blood and gray matter.

Once his target was prone in the dirt, Tran would lie on top of the fallen GI as if he were embracing him in a lover's grasp. Then he would touch the side of the man's throat with his index finger and, whenever he found a pulse, would wrap both hands around the neck, squeeze the carotid artery and choke off the flow of blood and oxygen to the brain.

Still smiling about his exploits, Tran was suddenly jolted back to reality by a distant rumbling. An airplane? he wondered. He scanned the night sky for the bright glow of landing lights but was unable to see anything. Still, he could hear engines quite clearly. Very likely another Russian cargo plan winging its way in from China, he thought. The plane's arrival meant they would have to unload more crates of AK-47s in the morning.

Barely above the treetops, the aircraft's black shadow was outlined by blue exhaust flames. Tran cocked an ear toward the sky and listened intently as the droning grew louder. Finally the plane swung even lower, the earth trembled underfoot from its roaring, and then it was gone.

THE GLOW OF THE INSTRUMENT PANEL painted the pilot's face red as he pointed through the windscreen. The copilot nodded, and one by one the flaming dots on the ground came into focus, forming an inverted L and marking the location of the drop zone.

In the rear of the plane the crew chief cupped his hands over the earphones so that he could hear the pilot's instructions. He nodded a couple of times, then peeled off the earphones and gave Gerber a thumbs-up.

Without a word the team members got to their feet and stretched stiff muscles. Then they shuffled single-file toward the ramp where they each picked up a parachute and lugged it back to their seats. Gerber flopped his onto his back like an oversize rucksack, then wriggled it into place. Chuted up, the tight harness forced him to stoop, as if he were an old man.

For the twentieth time Roland asked Gerber, "What altitude did you say we're jumping from?"

"Five hundred feet," Gerber said patiently, patting the staff sergeant on the chest directly over the vacant spot where the reserve chute would have been under normal circumstances "Don't forget," he added. "If you can walk away from it, it's a good jump." Then his grin broadened. "Of course, there are those who believe that if you can even crawl away, it's a good jump."

"Remember Africa and Fauber?" Fetterman asked solemnly.

Gerber's stomach knotted. How could he ever forget? Fauber had been a mutual friend from the early days of the Special Forces, back before the beret had been designated as official headgear, before President Kennedy had taken the SF under his protective wing. Back then, in the early days of Vietnam, the only American troops in the country had been a handful of Special

Forces advisers who weren't even supposed to carry firearms.

"Everybody gets butterflies before a jump," Fauber had told a famous French female journalist over a glass of wine. "Some guys get drunk the night before. Other guys go into town for what they're afraid will be their last piece of ass. We're not scared. We just know the risks."

The writer had probably been Fauber's last woman. Barely a week after the magazine interview, during a training jump with an ARVN airborne unit, Fauber had smacked hard into the Vietnamese soil when his main canopy hadn't opened.

Jumping from an accompanying aircraft, Gerber and Fetterman had already exited the aircraft and were descending earthward. They had looked on in horror as Fauber had whistled past, then had watched as he'd hit the ground and bounced four times before his broken body had settled in the red dust.

Gerber shook his head, trying to rid himself of old, memories. Because he was functioning as the jumpmaster, he leaned out the door of the aircraft and felt the warm rush of the prop blast.

Fetterman held on to Gerber's parachute harness to keep him from being sucked out by the slipstream "Can you see it?" he shouted over the earsplitting roar of the engines.

Gerber squinted into the prop wash past the starboard wing and engine. Below the plane rolled a carpet of treetops. Then he saw a meadow and the inverted L, the standard NATO drop zone marker. He smiled, swung back into the plane and shouted, "Stand up!"

Umber and Roland got up out of their troop seats, ready for the next command. Roland gulped and stretched his arm and leg muscles in anticipation of the imminent parachute drop.

"Hook up!" Gerber shouted, and all of the jumpers connected their static lines to the long steel wire that ran the length of the plane, careful that the open end of the hook pointed toward the skin of the aircraft. Then they pulled the opening closed and pushed the pen through the hook, locking it in place. The fifteen-foot-long umbilical cord would pull their parachute canopies out of the pack tray as they fell away from the plane. When it was fully deployed, the thread that tied the static line to the apex of the canopy would break, allowing the canopy to inflate with air.

"Sound off for equipment check," Gerber yelled. He checked each man in turn, carefully ensuring that the parachute harness wasn't twisted or improperly connected and that the static line was unobstructed in its stays. Then the pilot throttled back the engine, and the plane slowed to 120 knots, a speed that wouldn't tear the jumpers to pieces when they exited.

"Shuffle to the door," Gerber ordered, and the men moved in single file toward him. Gerber was surprised when Roland was the first man in the stick. "Thought you were afraid of jumping," he said.

"I am," Roland replied. "But I also like to face fear head-on, if you know what I mean."

Gerber nodded. "Stand in the door," he told the staff sergeant.

Roland assumed the position, his toes peeking out past the bottom of the door, his hands holding both edges of the doorway. Out of the corner of his eye he saw the red Get Ready light blink on. Finally the light changed to green.

"Go!" Gerber shouted.

Feet and knees together. Roland hurled himself into the night. All at once, the hot prop wash violently fluttered his jungle fatigues, and he could taste the oily exhaust fumes from the port aircraft engine as his parachute opened.

"Go, go, go, go!" Gerber yelled as Fetterman and Umber followed Roland in rapid succession. The closer they exited the aircraft to one another, the closer together they would land when they hit the ground.

Finally Gerber made his jump. When he looked up, he saw that he'd made a textbook exit from the aircraft. His canopy was fully deployed and none of the suspension lines had gotten tangled. So far, so good, he thought.

The team descended in a tight circle. In the moonlight their olive drab parachute canopies looked like dark clouds falling gently to earth. Ten feet from the ground, and with practiced skill, Gerber unhooked his parachute harness, hit the shoulder-high grass and rolled away with his rifle and ammo belt in hand. Now the fun would begin.

7

MILL RESTAURANT
IOWA CITY, IOWA

Jody March backed away from the beer tap, stuck his hands into his pockets and surveyed the evening crowd. The Mill Restaurant was a popular hangout in Iowa City, a watering hole for different occupations and political beliefs. A Mexican flag hung behind the bar above an aquarium that housed an enormous catfish named Hoover. The establishment was crammed wall to wall with church pews that had been converted into restaurant benches, and the edges of the tabletops were worn smooth from the countless anxious elbows that had rubbed against them over the years.

Tonight Juicy Joyce, a Joan Baez look-alike, stood onstage in front of the microphone, strumming an acoustic guitar and singing the story of union organizer Joe Hill in a low, sexy voice. Jody rocked back on his heels while he listened to the woman sing one sad folk song after another. As he listened, he scanned the audience, noticing some local musicians who were probably criticizing Joyce's performance as they studied her guitar picking and the nuances of her voice.

When Joyce's set ended and applause rippled through the room, she put down her guitar and bounced off the stage, her long black skirt billowing with every step she took. As he watched her go, Jody couldn't help admiring the woman's ample figure. She'd do nicely, he thought—any night, any time.

Directly in front of Jody the Tongue brothers sat on adjacent bar stools arguing good-naturedly about motorcycles. Jody had heard the argument a thousand times. In particular it revolved around whether or not Japanese bikes were about to take over the world. Both Tongues agreed that Honda was a dirty word, the name of a machine that threatened the sanctity of motorcycling and the American way of life.

The Tongues drove Harley-Davidsons. As far as they were concerned, there was no other motorcycles. With their shaggy hair, beefy arms, potbellies, tattoos and leather jackets, they looked like Hell's Angels. Indeed, the Tongues liked to horse around and drink beer all night, but they were generally good-natured no matter how intimidating they appeared to the other patrons of the restaurant. The raucous behavior was tolerated largely because they were good friends of the owners. The Tongues liked to drink and carouse. And when they weren't in the Mill, they were usually in their driveway, fooling around with transmissions and engine blocks.

"Hey, needlenose," the older Tongue, Rafe, called out to Jody in a friendly voice, "do you know the difference between a Mill waitress and a bowling ball?"

Jody winced. There were dozens of Mill waitress jokes, but he decided to play along. "No, what's the difference?"

"You could eat a bowling ball if you had to."

Jody grinned appropriately. It always paid to keep on the good side of the Tongues, even if they weren't actually Hell's Angels. Of course, no matter how funny a joke might be, Jody wasn't in a lighthearted mood these days. He had thousands of dollars worth of educational loans to pay back, and at the moment he was flat broke. Recently he had graduated from college with a degree in economics, but so far he hadn't been able to find a decent job. In fact, the only job he had been able to land was at the Mill Restaurant, tending bar. Of course, half of the people employed at the Mill were underemployed college graduates. Out of sheer desperation, Jody had only recently decided to return to school, which left him with one simple problem—how was he going to pay for tuition and books?

He scanned the dining room again, this time pausing when he came to Crystal Umber. He sighed as he looked at her. She was quite tall, standing five-nine, and was perfectly proportioned, neither too thin nor too big-boned. Whenever he looked directly into her blue eyes, Jody got a hard-on. She was the kind of a woman no one failed to notice.

Jody had heard through the grapevine that she was married and fooled around on her husband, who happened to be stationed overseas in Vietnam. And while Jody wasn't entirely convinced that the rumor was true, he hoped it was. Maybe someday he'd get the opportunity to find out firsthand.

Crystal and her group of twelve poet buddies were clustered around a table, smoking French cigarettes and drinking pitchers of cheap draft. The Mill was their regular Wednesday night hangout. If it hadn't been for Crystal, Jody would have let one of the waitresses serve them. The poets always seemed to have plenty of money for beer, but they never failed to stiff him on the tip. As far as Jody was concerned, though, talking to Crystal was tip enough.

One of the poets, a high-strung young man named Larry Lawrence, was quite drunk and talking too loudly. The jukebox was booming out a particularly loud Doors tune, so Jody couldn't make out the specifics of the conversation. Nevertheless, he figured he'd better keep an eye on Lawrence. The guy had caused disturbances before. Once he'd hurled a large glass ashtray through the restaurant's front window. And even though he'd apologized and paid for the replacement window the next day, the owner wanted Jody to watch the guy from now on.

The song on the jukebox ended, and the room was suddenly quieter. Larry pushed back his chair, stood up and began to spout free verse, presumably of his own composition. The other poets groaned, but Larry just stared at Crystal as he spoke, his booming voice echoing in the still room.

"Well," Larry said when he was finished, "did you like it?" He was still looking at Crystal. It was as if they were alone in the restaurant and no one else existed.

Crystal's face reddened, but Jody didn't know if it was from embarrassment or anger. Maybe it was both, with a little disgust thrown in for good measure.

"Hey, hippie," Rafe Tongue bellowed, "would you like to know my opinion of your poetry?" He didn't bother to wait for Larry's answer. Instead, he tilted back his head and belched loudly. "'Nuff said, I figure." Turning around, he took a deep pull of beer and wiped his mouth with the back of his hand.

Larry slammed both fists on the tabletop and up-ended a beer glass. Then he whirled around reached into his packsack and pulled out an automatic pistol.

Jody rolled his eyes and groaned. "Shit, not on my shift. Not again." A week before a woman had provoked a man into punching her right at the bar. The wife had gone to the hospital, the man to the county jail.

The Tongue brothers heard the commotion stirred up by Larry and turned around to see what was the matter. Rafe slapped his forehead and groaned. "Wonderful, now the raving idiot's going to commit bloody suicide." Then he chuckled and shook his head in disbelief.

"Don't laugh," Hoke, the younger brother, cracked. "I hear tell that after he kills himself, he's coming after you." Hoke slapped his brother on the back and devoted himself to more important matters, such as his beer.

Calmly Jody punched the No Sale key on the cash register, grabbed a handful of quarters, walked over to the jukebox and hurriedly punch up a dozen songs at random. It didn't matter in the least which ones he played. The music, he figured, would at least distract some of the attention from Larry, and the gun.

With the jukebox blaring, Jody walked directly over to Larry, making sure his arms hung down at his sides and that the expression on his face was pleasant, his body language as nonthreatening as possible. His jaw hurt with the effort to smile.

Larry pulled back the automatic's slide, then released it, chambering a round into the Colt .45.

"Brought this back from Nam," he said with pride. "Killed five Cong with it one night. Bang. Bang. Bang." He sighed meaningfully before continuing with his story. "Didn't want to, but it was them or me. War's a nasty business, you know."

Crystal's face was no longer red; it was now drained of all color. Still, she managed to pipe up, "Put your toy gun away, Larry. No one here's impressed with your war stories. You forget I've got a husband in Vietnam who writes me letters."

Larry pursed his lips and furrowed his brow. It was obvious that he was working hard to come up with a cute reply. Rocking back and forth, he finally said, "Yeah, Crystal, we can't forget your husband, but you forget him every night at closing time, if you know what I mean."

Crystal's face twitched, and her eyelids flickered as guilt rolled across her pretty features.

Jody figured Larry was relatively harmless, all wind and no punch. Still, it didn't pay to get careless with someone holding a gun, especially when he was drunk and a bit off center.

Then Larry worked the hammer and twirled the automatic. Jody grimaced and hoped the gun wasn't really loaded. As drunk as Larry was, he might accidentally fire the weapon and kill someone.

Larry grinned sloppily, raised the automatic and pointed it off into space, swinging it first to the left, then to the right. When the barrel of the gun swung around in his direction, one of the male poets dived out of his chair and hit the tiled floor hard. But Jody remained calm and asked Larry, "Is that a .45 automatic you've got there?"

The gun-toting drunk nodded.

Jody took a step closer. "I've only seen pictures of them in gun magazines and read articles about their stopping power. I've never really seen one close up, though. How did you say you got this one?"

Larry grinned. "Brought it back from Nam, man. I carried it for a year up and down the jungle trails. Saved my life more than once. It's like a brother to me."

Slowly Jody edged closer to Larry. By now he was so close he could reach out and touch him. He stared at the weapon, then pointed at it. "Wow, it's a 1911A1, isn't it?"

Larry pointed at the slide, where there were some markings. Proudly he said, "See here? It's even stamped Government Model."

Jody nodded. "So you saw a lot of action, huh? Must have been pretty rough over there." He hoped he wasn't overplaying his interest, because the last thing he wanted to do was alienate a man with a gun.

Larry sighed deeply for effect. "Yeah, it's still kind of hard to talk about. I was in the Marines. I'm the only guy out of my platoon who made it back alive." He paused before going on. "The others were, well, it's too difficult to talk about. You understand, don't you?"

Jody noted that the automatic had a blue finish and wasn't parkerized like a legitimate Army Colt. And while it was true that Government Model was stamped on the slide, there were no markings to indicate that it was now or ever had been Army property.

Clearly Larry was lying through his teeth. But truth, as it related to bogus war stories, wasn't the issue at hand. All Jody wanted to do was neutralize the tense situation as quickly as possible. "I've always wanted to hold a 1911A1," he finally said, pausing to let the idea sink into Larry's skull. Then he asked, injecting appropriate awe into his voice, "Gee, would you mind if I looked at it?"

Larry puffed out his chest. "Sure, go ahead."

The bartender slowly reached out a hand. Then, without warning, Larry pulled back, as if he'd changed his mind.

Softly Jody said, "Wow, what a neat gun. You must be quite a guy to have gone through all that action in Vietnam and come out alive."

Finally Larry handed the automatic to Jody, barrel first. Without hesitation the bartender expertly pushed the release button and dropped the loaded magazine into his free hand, pocketing it. The sheer weight of the magazine and ammo pulled at his pocket. Next, he worked the slide and ejected the live round from the chamber, catching it in midair. Then he breathed a sigh of relief. Now the gun was empty and the danger of violent death removed. But Jody wasn't through. In less than a minute he fieldstripped the weapon.

Larry's jaw dropped as he watched Jody. He seemed stunned that someone else could disassemble his .45 automatic.

When he was finished, Jody said calmly, "Listen, you're drunk. I'll lock this in the safe overnight. Come back tomorrow when you're sober and I'll give it back to you in pieces. In the meantime I want you to go outside, hop on your ten-speed bike, pedal your skinny ass home and sleep it off. Okay?"

Larry was nonplussed. All he would do was stand there working his jaw. Then Rafe slipped off his bar stool, walked over to Larry's chair and gathered up the man's packsack. By this time Hoke had joined him, and the two of them escorted Larry to the door. As the would-be poet slinked out the door, Rafe gave him a little push to help him on his way.

Jody walked back to the bar, his hands shaking as he began to wash some beer glasses and pitchers. With soapsuds up to his elbows, he heard Crystal's silky voice over his shoulder. "Jody, got a minute?"

He wiped his hands dry on his yellow bartender's vest and walked around to the end of the bar to meet her. She smiled demurely as she ran her fingers across the butterfly embroidered on his vest pocket. "I just wanted to thank you for dealing with that horrible situation. And I wanted you to know how brave I think you are. I'm impressed. Very, very impressed."

Jody shrugged. "It was nothing."

Crystal giggled. "Nothing? How modest!" She placed her hand on his shoulder, leaned forward and kissed him lightly on the lips. "A man with humility. How refreshing. And you're so handsome, too." She kissed him again, the time on the cheek.

Jody's pulse quickened. "Listen, I don't have to work tomorrow and there's a party I'm going to. Would you like to come with me? It's a Fourth of July picnic out at Monster's Christmas tree farm. There'll be lots of food and beer and we can watch the fireworks when they shoot them off in town."

"I'm married," Crystal said matter-of-factly. "So you realize it won't be like a real date or anything. Strictly platonic, okay?"

"Platonic," he repeated, his heart pounding. "Okay. We can still have some fun."

"Tomorrow then," she said, grabbing a bar napkin and a pen so that she could scribble down her address and phone number for him.

"Wait a minute," Jody said. "What about Larry Lawrence? What's he mean to you?"

Crystal giggled. "Larry? He's just one of the boys in my poetry workshop. I just made the mistake one night of inviting him over to read his poetry and have a glass of wine. He got the wrong idea somehow. You know how it is."

"Yeah," Jody said. "Guys will do that."

Just then one of the other poets called out to Crystal from the table. "Hey, Crystal, it's your turn to buy the beer."

She smiled, flipped her hair and walked back to the table. Jody wondered what adventures the next day would bring, but Rafe snapped him out of his reverie. "Hey, needlenose, I just saw you and that poet lady talking. Did she offer to give you a private reading of her poems?"

Jody nodded. "Yeah, sort of, I guess."

Rafe smirked. "You, too, huh? Well, listen, I liked the way you handled that idiot with the gun. He won't be back."

Jody shrugged. He was still thinking about Crystal. "It was nothing."

Rafe smiled. "Modesty will get you nowhere, but a chopper will." He stared at Jody, seeming to dare the bartender to inquire further.

Jody took the bait. "What do you mean?"

"You're taking the little lady to Monster's get-together tomorrow, right?"

"Yeah. That's the plan."

"And doesn't the lady in question have a husband off soldiering in Vietnam?"

"Right," Jody answered warily, wondering if Rafe was going to hassle him about dating a married woman whose husband was doing his patriotic duty.

"About the chopper," Rafe continued. "If you want to get in good with a lady, the recipe's simple: a Harley-Davidson never fails to impress. Take my word. You have to beat the babes off with a stick."

"Huh?" Jody, murmured, still failing to comprehend completely.

"It's simple. Show up at the party, then take the poet lady for a ride on my chopper. I'll leave the key in my saddlebags. Give the beast plenty of choke or she won't start. If that doesn't work, swear a blue streak at her. That'll usually coax her into life."

Jody stared at Rafe. Things were looking up. They were definitely looking up.

8

DROP ZONE FAUBER
NORTH VIETNAM

Lying flat on his back, Fetterman unfastened his parachute harness, then gathered everything up in a bundle and buried it. Consulting his compass, he found magnetic north, squinted in that direction and started walking until he bumped into Gerber, Roland and Umber. "Any casualties?" he asked Gerber, peering at the captain's blackened face. "Everybody in one piece?"

"No, Tony. Everyone came through without a scratch. For once," Gerber replied.

"What about the scouts? They turn up yet?"

Gerber pointed off in the darkness. "The road should be right about there. Let's find out."

But before they could take a single step, they heard the approach of footsteps. They all froze.

"Red dust," a voice with a heavy Vietnamese accent whispered. The password identified him as one of their Kit Carson scouts.

"Blue dust," Gerber countered, relaxing.

One of the men was tall for an Oriental, standing nearly five feet seven. The other was an average-sized Vietnamese.

"Welcome to my country, Captain," the tall one said as he smiled and extended a hand. "My name is Ngo, and this is Nguyen."

"Come," Nguyen, the shorter scout, said impatiently. "We go now." Without waiting for a reply, he spun around and started off down the pathway beaten through the tall grass.

Gerber nodded, and he and the other team members followed in the scout's footsteps, carefully maintaining intervals of ten meters to avoid complete annihilation if they fell into an ambush. About a klick farther on, they scurried up the side of a ditch and onto a gravel road, where they saw the faint outline of a truck—a Russian ZIL.

"Captain," Ngo said to Gerber, "we have no instructions where to go. You must tell us."

"I see." he answered. "You want to know where to take us?"

Ngo nodded.

From his study of the area's topography, Gerber knew the road they were facing ran north and south and that Son Tay, their target, was ten klicks to the south. He smiled at the tall scout and pointed north. "That way."

Fetterman overheard the conversation and understood its implication. Gerber didn't trust the scouts and was trying to test their loyalty somehow.

By now Nguyen had already lowered the truck's tailgate, and the Americans threw their packs onto the bed and then climbed in, taking seats along either side. Fetterman whispered to Gerber, "In the dark I'd swear this Commie rig was American-made."

"Uh-huh," Gerber mumbled. It was quite obvious he was preoccupied with something.

The front doors slammed and the engine started with a great deal of backfiring. The driver, Ngo, ground the gears until he found low, then dropped the clutch, killing the engine.

Gerber looked at Fetterman. "Okay, so it's not American-made," the master sergeant admitted.

A moment later the truck started to roll forward. Then Gerber suddenly beat his first on the back of the cab and ordered Ngo to stop. Motioning to Fetterman, he said, "Ride up front, Tony, and keep an eye on things. And send Nguyen back here with us."

"Yes, sir," Fetterman said. With AK-47 in hand, he scurried to the back of the truck and swung to the ground.

Gerber could hear the master sergeant's footsteps crunching in the gravel as he made his way up to the passenger door. Then Fetterman and the Vietnamese scouts bantered for a moment or two. Finally the door opened and a moment later Nguyen climbed into the back of the truck and sat down.

Even in the gloom, Gerber immediately noticed the sullen expression on the scout's face. Then the truck started off again. Gerber could feel the seething tension emanating from Nguyen in the back of the truck, and he was certain he could feel hostility in the way Ngo was driving the truck.

Gerber lay back against the canvas top of the truck and wondered what had really happened to Ngo and Nguyen's previous spike team. The Kit Carson scouts made him uneasy. He couldn't shake the feeling that they were leading him and his men into enemy hands.

After a while the truck started to slow, then stopped altogether. Nguyen became instantly alert. He raised his head and tightened his grip on his AK-47. Then Ngo beeped the horn twice.

Nguyen quickly unlatched the hooks on either side of the tailgate, dropped it with a clang, then leaped off the back of the truck. By now Fetterman and Ngo were standing behind the truck arguing heatedly.

"Down!" Ngo said. "Down!" he repeated, motioning for the Americans to join him behind the truck.

One by one the Special Forces troopers slipped off the tailgate. Gerber's stomach felt queasy. Intuition told him there was something very wrong going on. Since the drop zone, the scouts had been sullen and distant, not cooperative and friendly as they should have been.

Gerber leaned close to Fetterman. "What's the situation, Tony?"

Fetterman frowned. "They say we're supposed to wait here. Ngo won't say why or for how long. I'm trying to explain to him that to do that would leave us exposed. We need to get to where we're going or get under cover. I don't like sitting out here in the road like this, not behind enemy lines."

Gerber slipped the safety off his AK-47. "You thinking what I'm thinking, Tony?"

"I expect so, Captain. Ma Fetterman didn't raise any dummies."

"So, what do you suggest?"

"I'd say we don't have much choice. At least the odds are with us, though."

Gerber nodded, then murmured, "On the count of three."

Fetterman suppressed a grin, then called out to Roland, "Go check the engine oil at the front of the truck and don't ask any questions."

The staff sergeant looked stunned for the briefest of moments, then padded off. "Roger that."

The two scouts looked puzzled as their eyes followed Roland's progress to the front of the truck.

Gerber smiled. "Master Sergeant Fetterman."

"Yes, Captain?"

"Three."

They whirled around, took two steps until they were nose to nose with the scouts, then stuck the muzzles of their weapons in the faces of the Vietnamese. Wisely the scouts dropped their AKs and raised their hands, giving up without a hint of resistance.

Fetterman directed Umber and Roland to strip the rope from the truck's canvas and to bind the Vietnamese hand and foot, while Fetterman tore off the scouts' shirts and stuffed the thin fabric into their mouths.

The four Americans had barely stowed their captives in the back of the truck when they heard the unmuffled exhaust of another truck rolling down the steep grade. There were no headlights, just the dark form of the truck illuminated by moonlight.

"Looks like they're about a klick away," Gerber estimated.

"Fight or flight?" Fetterman asked.

"Too soon to tell. We'll have to play it by ear. In the meantime, blend into the bushes on either side of the road and stay awake."

The last thing Gerber did before taking cover was to set their truck's emergency brake, start the engine and shift the transmission into neutral. The phantom truck slowed, its brakes squealed, then it stopped. Nothing more happened for a few minutes. The only sounds came from the two ZILs idling side by side in the Road.

Gerber saw a muzzle-flash on the far side of the phantom truck, then heard a bullet hit the driver's side of their scouts' truck. Finally he heard a cough.

A moment later the passenger door of the new truck swung open and someone got out and walked over to the scouts' truck. The man shone a flashlight into the driver's compartment. Empty. Next he walked to the back of the truck and let the flashlight play on the bound and gagged Kit Carson scouts. Surprised, he barked out some commands in Vietnamese.

The rear tailgate on the other truck clanged down, and a dozen men piled out, encircling the scouts' truck. Amid the frenzied motion, Gerber could see that the newcomers were North Vietnamese regulars.

Gerber watched as the NVA untied Ngo and Nguyen and pulled the wadded-up shirts out of their mouths. The formerly sullen scouts became animated and started jabbering excitedly as they pointed up and down the road. The NVA with the flashlight shouted something at them, and the two scouts came to rigid attention and saluted.

Fetterman whispered, "Figure he's their superior officer?"

Gerber shook his head and held a finger to his lips. He was worried. If the scouts were traitors, they had probably told the NVA officer everything they knew. The officer would realize that Gerber and his men couldn't have gotten far in such a sort time. In that case their best chance was to open fire and wipe out as many enemy soldiers as possible before a search party was unleashed.

On the other hand, if the scouts were loyal, they would concoct some kind of story and the NVA would drive off, none the wiser. Gerber decided to wait. If the NVA started to search the roadside, that would be the trigger for the firefight. Twenty minutes later Gerber's patience paid off, and the NVA soldiers and the scouts drove off together.

"Looks like the scouts were on the up-and-up," Fetterman whispered. "But something about them still bothers me. I can't put my finger on it, though."

"I'm still not convinced they're on the up-and-up," Gerber said. "Besides, how do we know that little prick NVA officer didn't haul them off for intensive interrogation? If they suspect anything's out of line, their intel guys will separate the two scouts and go over their individual stories again and again. If they find any flaw, any difference between the two, they'll pick at it until they come up with something."

"You're right," Fetterman said worriedly. "If they find a flaw in their stories, they'll torture the poor bastards."

"For our own protection we might as well assume the scouts will betray us. It doesn't matter if they're on our side or not. No one can resist torture forever."

Umber gulped. "What will they do to them?"

Fetterman grimaced. "Depends on who's in charge. If it's an expert, they might mash their fingers with a sledgehammer. But if their interrogator's been trained in Moscow, he'll have a bit more finesse."

"Either way," Gerber added, "the end result's the same. They'll talk eventually."

Umber couldn't help his curiosity. "If the interrogator's been to Russia, what will he do to the Kit Carson scouts?"

Fetterman's tone of voice was deadly serious when he answered. "Again it depends. They might cover their faces with wet towels, then pour a steady stream of water over the nose and mouth. When they do that, every breath you take sucks in water. With your eyes blindfolded, it feels as if you're drowning. A lot of strong men crack."

Gerber agreed. "Every man has a breaking point."

"Shouldn't we at least try to bust these guys out?" Roland asked. "After all, they're assigned to our team. They're good guys, aren't they?"

Fetterman fielded the question. "Maybe," he said guardedly. "Unfortunately there's some question about their loyalty."

"Besides," Gerber added, "we've got a mission to accomplish. The scouts had bad luck. That's the way it goes sometimes. Ngo and Nguyen are on their own. Period."

"At least the scouts never knew our mission," Fetterman said. "They only knew to pick us up and guide us to where we were going. Good thing we were careful and had them run us in the wrong direction first."

"Yeah," Gerber said, "except that now we've lost a couple of hours and we'll have to hustle back in the opposite direction and get on with our mission."

Roland pointed at the truck. "I don't suppose we could take advantage of the resources we have at hand? Instead of walking we could ride—"

Gerber shook his head. "Oldest ruse in the book. If we take that truck, they'll know we were here. Face it, Staff Sergeant, we've got some serious humping to do in the next few hours."

Fetterman got to his feet and looked at Roland and Umber. "Come on, you two. Let's move it out."

9

NEAR SON TAY

Sergeants Roland and Umber stayed behind while Gerber and Fetterman reconnoitered the railyard staging area. Hidden in his nest, Umber monitored the radio, waiting for the call that would come from the SFOB at Nha Trang. Hearing the first string of dits and dahs, he adjusted the earphones and then grabbed his crypto pad and pencil. Methodically he copied the code that was transmitted as the series of Q and Z signals, three-letter abbreviations that could stand for entire sentences. With this sparse notation, transmission time was reduced significantly as was the possibility of error.

Once net control and Umber established that each end was in place and copying loud and clear, they got down to business. Umber told them they were on schedule and proceeding with the mission. Net control rogered his transmission and signed off. The whole exchange took less than thirty seconds.

With the necessary commo out of the way, Umber swept the frequency dial, looking for rock and roll, but was disappointed to find only love songs on the radio. "Jesus!" he muttered.

"What's the matter?" Roland asked.

"Goddamn radio stations. All they're playing is love songs. I feel like puking."

Roland nodded. "Makes you think about your wife, huh?"

"Yeah. We both like rock and roll."

"So what's the problem with Crystal, anyway? What are you so worried about?" Roland already knew what Umber would say; it was always the same drill.

"I don't know," Umber said. "It's nothing I can put my finger on exactly. It's just a feeling that she's not playing straight with me."

"Kind of like intuition, huh?"

"Yeah, that and a couple of other small details. Like just before I left for Oakland, I found a shoe box tucked back in the closet full of unpaid bills. Bills that I'd given her money for and that she said she'd paid. The electricity bill, rent and other stuff all in my name."

Roland shrugged. "So she's irresponsible with money. Lots of women are. Guys, too, for that matter.

Or maybe there's a reasonable explanation for what you found.''

Umber frowned. Roland could sense that he was mustering the courage to say something else. Finally he said, ''She also went on the pill.''

Roland shrugged. ''So? Lots of women are doing that.''

Umber looked him in the eye. ''Yeah, but not two weeks before their husband goes overseas for a year.''

Roland sighed. ''Oh, I see.'' After a minute he forced himself to say, ''Looks like you're in a tough situation, but cheer up. You're probably better off without her, anyway. All she does is make your life miserable.''

Umber turned off the radio and removed the headphones. ''I know I'm not the first guy. It's happened before. Some gal marries a guy for the monthly allotment, knowing he's heading into a combat zone. The broad gambles that sometime during that year he'll be killed and she'll end up with all that life insurance money to keep her company. Cold-hearted bitches. If the poor slob comes home, the woman simply files for divorce, and dumps him.''

Roland smiled sympathetically. To himself he thought the poor bugger is finally catching on. But a few minutes later he was thinking again about the Club Trópico back in Panama. Once more Anna, the Colombian beauty, was straddling him, her long black hair...

Then Umber nudged him, interrupting his reverie. Once the man had his attention, he pointed down the hill. Roland saw it immediately—a big Bengal tiger working its way through the tall grass and bamboo.

"Think he knows we're here?" Umber whispered.

Roland raised his head. "No, the wind's working for us. We're upwind. So he won't smell us. He won't see us, either. Tigers have an uncanny sense of smell but lousy vision. We'll just stay put and watch the show."

"What's he after? Can you see what he's after?" Umber whispered.

Roland didn't have to answer. The two men lay still in the tall grass at the top of the hill, watching as the tiger stalked a small deer. Flat on its belly, the huge cat worked forward carefully, pausing every few feet to sniff the wind. Soon the cat was ten yards from the deer.

Then, in one great motion, the tiger rose to its feet and covered the remaining distance in what seemed like a fraction of a second. The beast sprang onto the back of the deer, bringing it down immediately. Umber expected the kill to come quickly with a smash of a might paw against the deer's head, breaking its neck, or a crunching bite that would jam the tiger's teeth through the skull and into the brain. But nothing like that occurred.

Instead the tiger played with the deer, swatting it back and forth, letting it nearly get up onto its feet and then knocking it down again with a flick of one massive paw. Umber swore he could smell fear emanating from the deer.

Roland nudged Umber, then whispered, "From what you've told me about your wife, this tiger kind of reminds me of her technique. Just fucking with a guy to hear him make that sound, to hear him squeal. Difference is, the deer hasn't got a choice. You do. You can shrug that woman off your back anytime you want to."

"What do you mean?" Umber asked, not entirely sure he wanted to hear the answer.

"That tiger could kill the deer in a second. But from the look of things, it's not going to. It's just gonna keep right on fucking with it just to see it suffer, just to prolong its agony. Know what I mean?"

"Yeah, I know what you mean." Umber's mouth was as dry as sand.

Roland grinned. "Yeah, thought you might." The staff sergeant grabbed his AK and assumed the prone firing position. By now the deer was dead, and the tiger had begun to tear out big hunks of meat from its haunches.

Roland lined up the tiger's big, broad neck in his sights. "Enough's enough. Time for the curtain to fall on this performance." Then, taking a deep breath, he squeezed the trigger.

Umber thought he saw a faint puff of dust rise from the tiger's skin where the bullet hit. The beast whirled around and seemed to stare directly at the two soldiers.

"Goddamn puny AKs," Roland swore. "Good thing the son of a bitch isn't charging us." Again he took careful aim and squeezed the trigger.

This time Umber was sure he saw a puff of dust where the bullet impacted. The big cat stiffened. Then rolled over onto its side, pinning the dead deer to the ground.

"Chow time," Roland said. "Looks like the supermarket has a new stock of venison and tiger. How about we go help ourselves to it?"

Umber nodded, and they began the hundred-yard trek down the gently sloping hill. Five feet away from the kill, Roland held out an arm, cautioning Umber. "More than one hunter's been surprised by a tiger he thought was dead. Never take chances with a predator."

The staff sergeant circled the fallen animal until he faced it head-on. The tiger's eyes blinked, and it's nostrils flared.

Umber froze.

A fraction of a second later the tiger hoisted itself to its haunches, bared its yellow teeth and growled. With practiced skill, Roland dropped to one knee, took aim and fired. A second later the tiger's head jerked back, and a 7.62 mm hole opened up in its forehead, between its green eyes. The great beast slumped to the ground and let out a deep sigh.

"Now we know for sure the son of a bitch is dead," Roland grunted.

Umber took three quick steps until he was standing alongside his partner. "That was pretty close, wasn't it?"

"Yep," Roland said, unsheathing his knife. He stared intently at the layout of the two dead animals.

"This whole thing bothers me," Umber suddenly blurted out. "We've fired three shots in the past five minutes. Won't the NVA hear? Won't they come running to find out who's shooting?"

"No," Roland said, dismissing Umber's concern. "It's all a matter of perspective. You see, we're intruders. We're all hopped up and paranoid. If we fart, we worry the wrong pair of ears will hear it. But keep the North Vietnamese point of view in mind. A couple of scattered shots are a normal occurrence to them. We know we're here, but they don't know we're here. However, if they heard sustained bursts of automatic fire punctuated by a couple of hand grenades going off, then they'd come running. You see, it's kind of like robbing a bank. If you go busting into the place with a brace of sawed-off shotguns and a stocking cap pulled over your face, shoving and pushing customers and clerks, you're going to attract attention. But if you walk in all smiles, wearing a three-piece suit and act like you own the god-damn place, people are going to think you belong there."

Roland squatted, Ka-bar in hand, and began to slit open the deer's belly, keeping the blade in contact with the skin and avoiding the viscera. "Goddamn worthless knife," he grumbled. While the Ka-bar was good for taking out sentries, it's blade was clumsy at best when it came to skinning. It was just too big for the job.

Roland looked up at his partner. Umber seemed frozen in place. His eyes stared straight ahead, as if he'd been mesmerized.

"Hey, Umber, where are you? You're not thinking about that wife of yours again, are you?"

"Naw. I was thinking about something else."

"Uh-huh. And Ho Chi Minh is a cross-dresser who likes to sip pink champagne and dance the fucking tango with Mao Tse-tung."

Umber didn't answer.

Roland sighed. "What's going on, hoss? Do you want to tell me about it?"

After a moment Umber began to tell the story. "Me and Crystal were at a party back in Iowa City. Writers' workshop crowd from the university. We went to a poetry reading one night and then a bunch of us drove over to a professor's house afterward for some cheese and wine. Anyway, I'm standing there talking to Crystal and a couple of her so-called friends."

Umber's voice trailed off and his face flushed. After a moment he continued with his story, but it was obvious from the way his voice cracked that he was finding it difficult. "You see, when Crystal comes, she makes this little cooing sound. Very distinctive. Out of the blue some guy standing behind me started making the noise, just like Crystal does. This guy never said a word, just mimicked Crystal coming. I wanted to knock his teeth out, but I didn't want to make a scene. After a minute or so he got tired of the game and walked off."

"Bet you and she fought one hell of a battle when you got home."

"Yeah, Crystal and I had a big fight."

"Why did the asshole do that to you?"

"Why do you think? He'd obviously fucked my wife at some point and wanted to rub my nose in it."

"There's another possibility you might want to consider."

"Oh, what's that?"

"Maybe one of Crystal's old high school boyfriends told this yahoo all about her and he was just trying to get to you. Maybe he was jealous that you slept with Crystal and he never would. And even if that's not the case, you'll torture yourself a hell of a lot less if you believe what I'm telling you instead of figuring she's slept with the entire town."

"Yeah, I see your point," Umber said, but he didn't sound convinced.

"What's this woman got that gets you so worked up, anyway? Is she dynamite in the sack or something? Maybe you like to lick a woman's boots. Some guys do, you know."

"It's the way she looks, man," Umber explained. "It's her blue eyes. They say the eyes are a window into the soul, and I believe it. When I look into her eyes, I start to shudder. A hundred thousand butterflies flutter in my stomach. I can barely talk. The emotion's so strong I almost can't stand it. And when I take her into my arms and hold her close, it gets worse. When I kiss her, my blood boils. It feels like it's scorching the inside of my arms." Umber closed his eyes and rolled his head back, shaking it from side to side, no doubt savoring the image of his wife.

After a while he continued. "When we make love and she makes those little cooing sounds, well, some nights in the jungle I can't think about anything else. I guess there's no way to say what it really is. Crystal just gets to me, that's all."

"She gets to you, huh?" Roland muttered. "Makes you weak in the knees just to look at her? I think I understand." His voice took on an almost reverent tone. "I was married to a woman like that once. Her name was

Maureen.'' Absentmindedly he rubbed the bare ring finger on his left hand.

Umber didn't fail to notice the subconscious act. ''Did you ever have to worry about her being faithful?''

Roland shook his head. ''Nah. She wasn't that kind of woman, and I'm not the jealous sort. Doesn't matter. I never had to worry about her for a minute. Maureen was one okay lady.''

''So what happened? You're talking about her in the past tense. She must have caught you in the hay with some lady, right? And now she's married to a civilian.''

Roland responded with a noncommittal shrug, then said, ''You know how it goes.'' But he didn't elaborate.

Instead, he drifted into a deep reverie, savoring the memory of his wife and twin boys on the snowy morning when things had gone horribly wrong. At first light the two boys had raced down the stairs, thinking it was Christmas morning, but they were one day early and were shocked to see the emptiness beneath the Christmas tree. All of Santa's presents were still hidden in the attic.

Slowly and tearfully the twins climbed back upstairs to wake up their parents. Little Bobby shook Maureen awake, complaining, ''Oh, Mom, Santa didn't come and he didn't leave any toys. I know I've been bad, but I didn't know I was that bad.''

The next morning the twins were happier. By then Santa Claus had dropped off shiny tricycles and race car sets, baseballs and catcher's mitts. Roland, who had pitched on his high school team, remembered how he had warmed up the two boys for the major leagues with a cautious game of catch in the living room.

At the stroke of noon Maureen served up the traditional Christmas dinner of turkey, sweet potatoes and pecan pie. Afterward, Roland sacked out on the couch while Maureen drove herself and the kids over to her sister's house for a quick visit. At the intersection two blocks from home a drunk in a Cadillac crushed Maureen's Austin Mini as if it were a bug. The twins died instantly.

In the emergency room Roland held Maureen's hand while the hospital staff fought to save her life. A skinny X-ray girl ran bloody cassettes through processing so that Dr. Buckman could see which bones weren't broken.

"Move your fingers for us, Maureen," the doctor coaxed. But Maureen couldn't move anything.

The doctor helped the technician slide Maureen into position for the next series of X rays. "Hold it, hold it," the technician said. Blood smeared the front of her surgical gown. Roland couldn't help remembering how ghoulish it made her seem.

The ambulance driver looked on. "Glad it's her pain," he mumbled.

Dr. Buckman was explaining the craniotomy procedure to Roland when Maureen's heart ruptured. Without warning, blood gushed from her mouth. In horror Roland looked on as his wife bled to death and drowned in her blood at the same time. Roland never forgot the look of terror in her eyes that Christmas morning when the world had gone black.

Now, in Vietnam, he called out, "Hey, Frank, are you a drinking man?"

"Not particularly, no. Why do you ask?"

"You ever drive drunk?" Roland pressed.

Umber could tell by the staff sergeant's tone of voice that this was a loaded question. "No, I'd never do that. Why do you ask?"

"Oh, nothing in particular. Just trying to get a fix on you, that's all. You see, I drink but not to excess. And I hate drunks."

By then they had wrapped tiger and venison in leaves and had started back up the side of the hill. Roland wondered if Umber could hold his emotions together long enough to survive the mission. Then he wondered if he could. They sure as hell made a great pair.

10

HILLTOP OVERLOOKING SON TAY

Gerber and Fetterman lay on their bellies, surveying the valley from south to north. High above the hazy blue horizon the sun beat down with intense heat. Fetterman wiped his sleeve across his forehead, soaking up a gallon of sweat with the shirt's fabric. It was one hot mother, he mused, holding his hand out to shield his eyes against the glare. His stomach grumbled, but he ignored it. He wished he'd eaten more back in the isolation compound.

Even though the railyard and fueling complex was camouflaged against the threat of B-52 arc light raids, Fetterman was able to see the layout and activity before them in incredible detail. A mosquito buzzed his ear, and Fetterman slapped it away, then reached down to rub his legs. The calf muscles ached from the long trek the night before.

Then the master sergeant heard a familiar chugging, smelled woodsmoke and could see an orange glow in the yard. "Look at that," he said. "And honest-to-God steam locomotive. Haven't seen one of those since I was a kid." Then Fetterman pointed it out so that Gerber could also appreciate its mechanical beauty.

The two men watched in silence as the black engine worked in the yard, nudging boxcars together to form a train that would obviously be hitched to a diesel for the trip south. The way Fetterman had it figured, the steam engine stayed in the yard and was used as a switching engine. And that made sense, because an ancient engine was likely to break down often and would be much easier to fix near a machine shop than a hundred miles from nowhere.

"I've always had this thing about steam engines," Fetterman told Gerber. "One Christmas my dad gave me a book about railroading. He was an engineer on the Chicago and Northwestern. Did you know toward the end of the last century they'd get two steam engines going full blast from opposite directions so that they'd slam into each other at top speed? Of course, they sold tickets and hot dogs and soda pop to the crowds. When the two locomotives smashed head-on, the sound of the crash was tremendous. You could hear it for miles.

When the boilers blew up, they scattered cast-iron shrapnel all across the countryside."

Gerber nodded. "Must have been quite a spectacle. Who sponsored it? Not the railroad, I hope."

"Nah. The fucking newspapers. Circulation drives."

Gerber sighed in disgust. "Figures. Things haven't changed in a hundred years. If it's a slow news day, they'll manufacture stories or twist the truth so that it's more palatable. Anything to whet the public's appetite so they'll cough up some spare change for newsprint. You know, Tony, we'll have to blow up that locomotive tomorrow, antique or not."

"Yeah," Fetterman said a little sadly. "War is war." He resumed his binocular inspection of the area, studying terrain, buildings and fortifications. Then he and Gerber discussed the strengths and weaknesses of various strategies until they settled on a plan of attack.

From down in the valley came a familiar echo—a single gunshot. Gerber and Fetterman stiffened and looked at each other. A few moments later another shot rang out. Finally, five minutes later, a third shot broke the relative silence.

Fetterman was the first to speak. "What do you think, Captain? Think our guys ran into trouble?"

"Maybe. I mean, what else could it be?"

"A coincidence?"

"Let's run through it."

"All right."

"First, we know when the North Vietnamese chase downed pilots they send position reports by firing off single shots in a particular sequence."

"Yeah, okay. Different sequences indicate direction and movement."

"And here we are in North Vietnam, deep behind enemy lines, and we hear what sounds like a shot pattern."

"So what do we do?"

Gerber shrugged. "There's only one thing we can do. We finish the recon and then get back to Roland and Umber and assess the situation. The NVA could be after another spike team, but the very fact that they're out in the boonies looking for somebody increases the odds that they'll stumble across us by accident. And we wouldn't want that to happen, would we?"

Fetterman grinned. "No, sir, we wouldn't. We sure as hell wouldn't."

After they finished the recon, Gerber and Fetterman made their way back to the assembly point. When they got there, Fetterman could see how Umber and Roland had made a little fire that gave off barely a trace of smoke. The few wisps of smoke there were ran into a roof woven from reeds and supported by a lean-to frame.

"Umber," Fetterman said, "I want you to get on the radio and sweep the frequencies the NVA use. We're looking for any activity that indicates they've got units in the immediate area searching for downed pilots." He paused for a moment. "Or looking for a spike team."

"Like us, you mean?" Roland asked.

"Yeah, like us," Gerber piped in.

"What happened?" Roland asked. "Something spook you guys out there?"

"The NVA fired shots into the air," Gerber said. "Typical pattern for them. They'll fire a shot, wait a minute, then fire another. Five or ten minutes later they'll shoot off one or two more. The sequence varies. It's like a Morse code. They use it to communicate between ground units."

Roland and Umber looked at each other.

Gerber continued. "Usually they do it when they're hot on the heels of a downed flyer or a spike team. But given last night's incident with the NVA regulars and the trucks—"

"Uh, Captain," Roland interrupted, "this is kind of embarrassing. No, not kind of. It's very embarrassing. I fired those shots."

"Oh?" Gerber said, frowning. "Why? At what? Did you have to take out some NVA or local militia?"

Roland closed his eyes. "No. The shots weren't fired in anger. I shot a tiger that killed a deer. That's the meat cooking there."

Gerber's mouth fell open, and Fetterman nearly dropped his AK-47 onto the ground.

"You did what?" Gerber growled, his face flushing. He was fighting to control the anger welling up inside.

"I shot a tiger."

Gerber rolled his eyes and swore. "You took the chance of jeopardizing the entire mission just because you had to take a potshot at a goddamn tiger? Christ, man, you're a professional soldier. What were you thinking of?"

"I wasn't thinking, Captain. I just wasn't thinking, that's all. Not that it will help any, but I apologize for my stupidity."

Gerber sighed. "Well, the damage is done, if there is any. I expect all we can do is go ahead with our plan. We'll move out at dark."

The Green Beret Captain turned his attention to Umber, who had the headphones on and was flipping through the band. "What's up, Umber? Who's talking and what are they saying?"

"Nothing out of the ordinary, Captain. Just routine chatter." Umber was more than a little nervous. After all, he had been part of the great tiger hunting safari.

Fetterman sensed Umber's distress and spoke to him in a calm, reassuring voice. "Stay on the radio for a while, Sergeant. Keep monitoring. You hear anything we should know about—"

"Roger that," Umber replied.

Gerber glared at Roland. "I hope you can restrain your great white hunter tendencies and save your ammo for the enemy. Anyone can make a mistake, but the problem is that in our line of work mistakes kill people."

"I know, Captain. I'm sorry. I really am. It won't happen again."

"Good," Gerber said. "See that it doesn't. You were lucky this time. It looks like the enemy didn't notice anything." He looked at the fire. "Well, since you've bagged us some meat, I guess we might as well chow down. It might be a while before we get the chance again."

Fetterman grinned. "Sounds good to me. Anything's better than C-rats."

"Never had tiger meat," Gerber admitted. "They say it tastes like chicken."

"So I've heard," Roland said, cheering up a bit as he poked a stick in the glowing embers.

"Well, let's eat and get that fire out," Gerber said, looking around nervously. "No matter how well you made that fire, it's dangerous to be cooking anything."

The men smacked their lips and dug in. As Gerber helped himself to some tiger meat, he couldn't avoid thinking that it might be the last meal he'd ever eat. Somehow the incongruity of the situation alleviated his tension. Welcome to Uncle Ho's Palace, he thought. Specialty of the house—tiger steak, and death.

11

SON TAY INTELLIGENCE COMPOUND

The military adviser's rippling chest muscles strained the fabric of his white T-shirt, which bore the CIA emblem—a blue circle, a bald eagle, a red starburst and the motto, And the Truth Shall Set Ye Free. Though Russian born and raised in Leningrad, the blond man with the hard blue eyes had a sense of humor.

But tonight his thoughts were focused on two prisoners the militia had brought in. A routine patrol had picked them up, bound and gagged, on a gravel road in the middle of nowhere without a good explanation why they were there. Major Tokarev suspected they had something to do with an American spike team, and somehow things had gone wrong. What other possible explanation could there be? he thought as he put on his lab coat.

Under Tokarev's direct orders, Ngo had been strapped naked to a stainless-steel autopsy table in the interrogation room. In order to maintain his sanity and diminish his fear while he waited for the interrogation to begin, Ngo counted the cracks in the wall. Then, suddenly, he felt the interrogator's fingers grip his arm. Looking up, he saw a Russian wearing a white lab coat.

Tokarev was a proud man. He had attended the Tblisi school that taught one to rely on technique, not outmoded brutality. In the modern world there was no need for hand claws to scrape out eyeballs. Tokarev compared himself to a scrubbed surgeon who used intelligence and training to remove a tumor from a patient.

In Tokarev's experience patience worked best. Haste all too often killed a man prematurely. Dead prisoners told no tales, but a frightened one could be counted on to give names, troop numbers and mission details. This man would talk. Soon he would beg for a chance to spill everything he knew. But first, Tokarev reflected, you had to make sure you had your subject's undivided attention.

The guards dragged in Ngo's companion whose face looked like a side of raw beef. Without saying anything, Tokarev drew his pistol, stuck the muzzle next to the shorter Kit Carson scout's temple and pulled the trigger.

Ngo's heart stopped for two full beats, then he realized the firing pin had fallen on an empty chamber. Tokarev and the guards laughed. Then the Russian worked the slide on his autoloader and placed the muzzle against Nguyen's head a second time.

The scout closed his eyes and braced himself for the inevitable. This time the gun went off, and the impact of the bullet viciously snapped his neck to one side as gray matter and bits of bone splattered the opposite wall.

Tokarev ordered the guards to drag the body out of the room. Then he leaned over the table and looked Ngo in the eye. "You're next if you don't tell me what I want to know," he said in Vietnamese. "Will you cooperate?"

Ngo closed his eyes and pressed his lips together.

The message was obvious to the Russian. This man would take work. Usually shooting a man's comrade shook the survivor enough so that he blurted out everything he knew to avoid the next bullet. But not this one. No matter, Tokarev thought. Now he could pursue the kind of work he loved best. "Do you swim, Comrade?" he asked.

Ngo didn't answer.

"Still silent, eh? Well, we'll see what we can do about that." With a wave of his hand, he ordered the guards to wrap Ngo's face with wet towels. "Be sure to cover his nose and mouth and wrap them tightly so that he has to breathe in the water.''

After the guards had done as they were told, Tokarev ordered them to pour buckets of water on Ngo's face. With the wet towels masking his mouth and nose, the scout inhaled vaporized water and felt as if he were drowning.

Tokarev waved away the bucket brigade. ''Your name, Comrade. What is your name?''

Once more Ngo remained silent. He watched as a guard splashed one of the unused buckets of water against the wall, washing Nguyen's blood and brains off.

When Ngo wouldn't talk, Tokarev slapped him. ''Pour the water again. He'll talk or drown.''

The two attending NVA soldiers slowly poured buckets of water on Ngo's covered face. The drowning sensation got worse as water clouded the scout's lungs. He bucked like a bronco, panic growing inside him every second.

He'll talk, Tokarev thought. Was he here to blow up an ammo dump? To run an intelligence-gathering mission for the CIA? Whatever the answer, soon everything would be clear. That was always the way.

At Tokarev's direction the guards took turns emptying buckets of water over Ngo's head until the floor was slippery. Ngo bucked, coughed and spit as the water filled his mouth and nose and mist choked his lungs.

Finally, after what seemed like hours, the soldiers stopped pouring.

Tokarev chuckled as the soldiers unwrapped Ngo's face and flipped the soggy towels onto the floor. "Ready to talk? Or would you rather drown in your own spit?"

Ngo nodded weakly, indicating he'd had enough.

"Perfect," Tokarev said with a satisfied grin.

Ngo motioned to Tokarev, and the Russian knelt next to him. "I'll talk," he whispered. "But alone." He pointed at the two soldiers. "I don't want anyone to see me like this."

Tokarev considered the request for a moment, then ordered the soldiers out of the room. "Wait until I call for you," he told them as they exited. Then he pulled out a notepad and pen. "What is your mission? Are you working for the CIA?"

Ngo remained silent and stared at the pack of cigarettes in Tokarev's lab coat pocket.

"What is your mission?" Tokarev pressed. Then he noticed the object of Ngo's gaze. "Oh, of course." He put his notepad and pen on his lap and reached for his cigarettes. Tapping one out, he lit it and stuck it between Ngo's lips. That done, he picked up his notepad and pen again and continued. "As you can see, we're not all that bad. When you've finished telling me everything you know, we'll feed you and really make you feel welcome. Now, tell me why you're here."

Ngo tried to answer, but with the cigarette in his mouth it was impossible.

Tokarev sighed. "How foolish of me." He unfastened Ngo's right arm.

Before Tokarev could react, Ngo's fingers encircled his throat. Then, smashing his own forehead against the Russian's Ngo stunned the torturer. After a few seconds without oxygen, Tokarev slipped into unconsciousness and crumpled to the floor.

Ngo untied the other straps, then slid off the table. He looked down at the unconscious Tokarev and scowled. Flipping the man onto the autopsy table, he strapped him down. Next he searched the room for something long, thin and pointed. When he found an ice pick, he walked over to the table and slapped Tokarev into consciousness.

The Russian's eyes opened wide when he saw Ngo standing over him. "Now it's my turn, you Russian pig." Ngo jabbed the ice pick into Tokarev's cheek just below the eye and next to the nose. Then he wriggled the point of the pick through the flesh until he hit bone. Tokarev didn't even whimper.

"You're a very brave pig," Ngo said, "but wait until I really begin my torture techniques. Then we'll see how brave Russians really are."

Ngo probed the cheekbone for a certain nerve. When Tokarev screamed, he knew he'd found it. As Ngo continued to jab the nerve, Tokarev's screams rattled the walls.

Outside the interrogation room door, the guards heard the screams but assumed they came from Ngo. Besides, they had orders to wait until further notice.

When Tokarev became hoarse from all the screaming, Ngo stopped and began to ask the Russian questions. Tokarev told the Kit Carson scout everything he knew about Son Tay. Most important, Ngo found out how he could escape from the compound.

Not it was time to move. Without further ado, Ngo cut the Russian's throat, then retrieved his clothes from the corner of the room and put them on. Next he took Tokarev's automatic pistol, dumped the magazine and noted, with appreciation, the hollowpoint rounds. He considered what he had just been told by the Russian and figured he had a good chance of getting out alive. Smiling grimly, he reloaded the pistol, then rapped on the door to get the attention of the two guards. "Come in now," he mumbled.

The soldiers sauntered in, oblivious to what had just happened to Tokarev. Ngo's gun bucked and the hollowpoint slug caught the first guard in the chest. His next shot hit the other guard in the hip, the impact wheeling his around. Then Ngo fired again, and the slug smashed into the man's skull. Without hesitating, Ngo raced out the door and into the night.

12

SON TAY RAILYARD

Gerber and Fetterman watched the second hands of their government-issue watches. They were hidden in the bushes just beyond the track bed, watching a slow-moving train roll by. An hour before first light the two Green Berets made their move.

Matching the speed of the freight cars rolling along the rails, they ran along the tracks. Then Fetterman grabbed the side of an open boxcar and heaved himself aboard, with Gerber following suit.

The two men rode the train southward, first passing the outskirts of the railyard, then gliding directly into the yard proper. Twice they spotted roving pairs of guards walking between the tracks, sleepy-eyed and bored, never expecting to see intruders. The guards failed to notice the huddled shapes of the two men inside the boxcar.

Once they were deep into the compound, Gerber saw their landmark and nudged Fetterman, who nodded in silent acknowledgment. Using a routine they had employed dozens of times before, Gerber tapped Fetterman's back three times. On the third tap the two men leaped from the train. When the balls of their feet hit the gravel, they tumbled and rolled to prevent broken bones or sprained ankles.

The two soldiers rested on the gravel, looking and listening for guards. After a few minutes, satisfied that no one had seen or heard them, they scurried up the side of the hill.

When they neared the crest, they began to run diagonally, as if following a ridge line. Soon Fetterman could see the faint outline of a sandbagged emplacment. Now they were crawling three and four yards at a time, then stopping to look and listen. Again, once they were satisfied that nothing was amiss, they started to crawl closer to their objective. With infinite patience, they took half an hour to cover the hundred yards, then positioned themselves with their backs against the sandbags on either side of the emplacement's single doorway.

Gerber held up his hand, and Fetterman could see the dim outline of the captain's fingers as he counted off the familiar sequence. On three, the two men rushed into the bunker, brandishing their Ka-bars.

Three North Vietnamese soldiers were on duty. Two were asleep, with their chins on the chests. The other man was groggy. When he heard Gerber and Fetterman rushing in, he stumbled to his feet, expecting to encounter an officer inspecting the guard post.

Instead, a dark figure loomed before him, and he felt an intense pain in his solar plexus as a Ka-bar blade penetrated his lung and pushed through to his heart. Gerber grabbed the man by his left lapel, controlling the gradual slide of the fresh corpse to the bunker floor. Meanwhile, Fetterman dispatched the sleeping guards, and soon the bunker was securely in their hands.

"So far so good," Fetterman whispered.

"So far," Gerber responded guardedly.

The two Green Berets took stock of the situation. The bunker was located on a high vista and seemed to overlook the whole valley. Below them they could clearly see the railyard clogged with boxcars and a sprinkling of diesel engines.

Fetterman watched intently as the steam locomotive huffed and puffed, helping to put together a string of cars. On the other side of the valley and halfway up a hill were the dark, round shapes of the tank farm and the millions of gallons of petroleum products.

Gerber checked his watch. "Nearly show time. We better get busy."

They started with the heavy 12.7 mm machine gun, making certain the piece was operational and not red-lined. Next they began opening crates of ammunition so that changing belts on the 12.7 would be easy once the fireworks started. That done, they began to take inventory of the other items in the bunker.

"What should I do with the phone?" Fetterman asked. "If we tear out the wires, they might run a continuity check and come looking for the break in the line."

Gerber nodded. "Yes. And if we leave it alone and it rings when the little bastards run a commo check and no one answers, we're still fucked. So I guess we follow the sage advice of General Montgomery."

"Oh, what's that?"

"When in doubt, do absolutely nothing."

"Sounds more like something you'd read in Chairman Mao's little red book."

"You're referring to his commentary on battles, right? Never engage in a battle you're not absolutely positive you can win."

"Yeah," Fetterman said. "I wonder sometimes about the battles we get ourselves involved in. Most of the time we string things out pretty thin."

Gerber grinned. "You mean like this mission and all
the missions our friend Jerry Maxwell dreams up for
us?"

"Yeah," Fetterman grunted as he unloaded an RPG-
2 rocket launcher.

"It's our job to take stupid chances," Gerber said.

Fetterman nodded. "True. It's our job. But there's
more at stake. Back in isolation I heard Maxwell ask you
why you still run these direct-action missions. Heard
him ask why you—"

Gerber interrupted. "I told him I liked it because
being close to death makes me feel alive. How about you,
Tony? You've been doing this sort of thing since D-day.
Maybe you should hang up your M-16 and ride a desk."

Fetterman loaded a rocket into the launcher and poked
it out one of the observation ports. "Bite your tongue.
The day I jockey a desk will be the day General West-
moreland turns up in Saigon wearing a dress. You've
heard that old saying about old soldiers dying with the
boots on? Well, this old soldier will die with his helmet
on and his Ka-bar in his hand."

"Not to mention your boots on a few NVA heads,"
Gerber cracked.

The two men sat in silence for a while on bamboo
chairs, looking out of the observation port and watching the steam engine chug back and forth. Then Fetterman leaned back in his chair and let out a relaxed sigh.

"Kind of reminds me of sitting on my grandmother's porch, watching the cars going down the highway in the summer. All we need is some Beam's and a couple of pretty ladies to keep us company."

Gerber nodded, then wondered how Roland and Umber were doing. He hoped they weren't playing safari again.

ON THE FAR SIDE of the valley Umber and Roland made their way down the reverse slope of the hill directly behind the fuel dump. Under cover of darkness they watched for trip wires, depressions in the ground or weeds tied back, all certain indications of booby traps or land mines. Carefully they picked their way over the terrain, ready to freeze in their tracks at the slightest suspicion.

When they got to the base of the hill, the terrain changed. The grass had been cut by machete, and the stench of diesel fuel from leaks and spills permeated the air.

With no more concern than if he were on the parade field behind the School of the Americas barracks at Fort Gulick in the Panama Canal Zone, Roland paced off the distance from the last row of tanks forward to the first row of tanks that overlooked the valley and the railyard below. Then he shook his head. It never ceased to amaze him how accurate intel photos could be.

Umber stood at his elbow and whispered, "What do you want me to do now?"

"Here, help me," Roland answered as he squatted and prepared to place the initial charge. First he estimated the thickness of the tank's steel plating. Then he calculated how much C-4 it would take to cut through the steel. Next he figured out the necessary weight for the charge, then added a little more C-4 for good measure. He had learned long ago that it was always better to detonate too much explosive than not enough, especially when your life depended on the blast working the first time. Finally Roland finished up by pressing an electric detonator into the lump of plastique.

That completed, the two Green Berets wired up each fuel tank in turn, connecting them with primer cord. When they were finished, they beat a retreat back up the hill where they would be safe from primary and secondary blasts.

Taking cover behind a fallen log, the two men stretched out and relaxed. Roland looked at Umber. In the moonlight he could clearly see the younger man's face and could tell he was nervous. "Thinking about your wife again?"

"Who?" Umber mumbled, his mind fixed on the impending explosion.

Roland just shook his head and made himself comfortable.

13

SON TAY RAILYARD

"Now?" Fetterman asked impatiently.

"Why not?" Gerber replied.

The master sergeant took the RPG-2 launcher in hand, raised it to his shoulder and stared down the sight until he had a boxcar lined up. Then he squeezed the trigger and a rocket whooshed out. A couple of seconds later the party began.

Fetterman's aim had been a little off, and instead of striking the boxcar broadside, the rocket hit the railbed. The explosion twisted a length of rail and scattered a great deal of gravel. Two guards who had been patrolling ten yards away were torn to pieces by bits of rock and shards of steel. When the track and railbed collapsed, the boxcar tipped over onto its side, twisting the cars on either side.

Gerber laughed. "Good shooting, Tex."

Fetterman frowned. "I never said I was Annie Oakley."

"I bet Annie never fired off an RPG," Gerber allowed.

Fetterman busied himself with reloading the launcher for a second shot. The first rocket had roused the sleepers, and soon NVA soldiers started pouring out of the barracks. Most of them carried AK-47s in one hand and bandoliers of ammo in the other.

Both Green Berets ignored the potential attackers and concentrated on taking out the railroad equipment, which was their objective. Gerber fired off the 12.7 and watched as red tracers arced across the sky toward the boxcars. Even from a distance he could see splinters fly as the big bullets tore into the wood. Then, without warning, the car disintegrated. Where moments before there had been splinters, now there were large chunks of wood hurled into the air, propelled by a strange orange-white blossom of light.

Gerber dived onto the floor of the bunker and covered the back of his head with his arms. "Duck!" he yelled.

Fetterman hit the dirt a millisecond before the clattering started. Hundreds of pieces of boxcar and torn-up ammo crates hammered the bunker. The shock wave blew in through the observation port, warming the cool, damp air momentarily. Then came the sound wave, a very loud, dull roar that shook the ground like an earthquake.

When the danger was over, Gerber and Fetterman stared out the window. Where the boxcar had once stood there now lay only wreckage. The adjacent cars were in various stages of destruction, some missing roofs, others walls and doors. The cargo lay scattered along the track bed as if some giant hand had thrown a temper tantrum and wreaked havoc. Some of the cars were burning furiously, and ammunition was starting to cook off.

"Let's get back to work," Gerber said, settling in behind the machine gun. A moment later he was firing off 5-round bursts, bracketing his shots until he was on target. Then he used the big bullets to tear up the sides of the railroad cards. He noticed how the tracers and incendiary bullets started little fires of their own. "Got any more rockets?" he called out to Fetterman.

"As a matter of fact, Annie's about to give Hiroshima a run for its money," Fetterman rasped. He pointed the RPG out the window. The locomotive was moving as fast as it could from the conflagration. The master sergeant knew he would have to fire quickly or it would soon move out of range. He relaxed and pulled the trigger, but nothing happened. He squeezed the trigger again. Still nothing. Swearing, he brought the launcher down from his shoulder and replaced the dud with a fresh rocket. This time, when he pulled the trigger, the rocket motor fired and delivered the projectile in a slow, sweeping path.

Once more his aim was too low, and the rocket hit one of the rails a hundred yards in front of the locomotive. The explosion split the rail in half and curled it back on itself.

Fetterman could clearly see the engineer in the cab slam on the brakes. The sudden move threw him to the floor of the locomotive as he attempted to stop in time to avoid derailing. Now the locomotive was a sitting duck. "I need some backup here," Fetterman called out.

Gerber nodded and lined up the machine gun with the locomotive. He had already fired off three boxes of 12.7 mm ammo and was getting pretty good with the gun. He also knew exactly what would happen when the armor-piercing bullets started slamming into the engine's boiler. Since the engineer and his fireman had been trying to make maximum steam, they had stoked the boiler, increasing pressure to a critical level. The boiler was a bomb waiting for detonation.

"Give my regards to Karl Marx," Gerber growled.

Fetterman watched as the locomotive ground to a halt in front of the broken rails. The engineer tried frantically to throw the engine into reverse, and the iron horse began to back away slowly from the bent rails. Then a string of red tracers from the 12.7 danced across the sky.

Realizing what was about to happen, the engineer and fireman leaped from the cab and took off, running in the opposite direction. The locomotive was still in reverse and picking up steam.

From a thousand yards away Fetterman could hear the loud clamor that the 12.7 mm bullets made as they struck the cast-iron boiler. Then one of the armor-piercing rounds punched through the side and steam shot into the air.

Gerber fired a long burst at the locomotive as it rolled backward. A dozen holes opened up in the boiler, spewing tiny clouds of steam. Then one great cloud issued forth, masking the entire engine. Big hunks of steel and rivets hurtled through the air.

"Hit the deck!" Gerber shouted, hurling himself to the floor.

Fetterman stayed in place until the last possible second, watching as the debris sliced through telegraph poles and decapitated the engineer and fireman. Then the master sergeant joined Gerber on the floor.

Shrapnel thudded into the sandbags, and one large piece of plate hurtled through the window and smacked the wall behind them. Fetterman looked at Gerber. "We should have taken pictures. We could have sold them to the newspapers."

Now the bunker was taking small-arms fire. A flurry of bullets slammed into the sandbagged walls as the defending troops began to fire back.

Gerber crawled over to the machine gun, keeping low in case a lucky shot squeezed in through one of the bunker's firing ports. He knocked his bamboo chair out of the way and crouched behind the big weapon. Then he began firing belts of ammo. This time he fired at men and not machines. The big bullets slammed into the front of one NVA trooper, knocking a gaping hole in his back and tearing out his spine.

One NVA's head was knocked clean off. Other enemy troopers had their arms, legs and hands ripped from their bodies as the 12.7 mm bullets smashed bones and tore flesh.

Fetterman finished reloading the RPG and poked it outside. Carefully he took aim on a red-and-black diesel locomotive that was chugging northward in an obvious escape attempt. Recalling the results of his last two shots, he raised his aim, then squeezed the trigger. The rocket whooshed across the valley. "Come on, you son of a bitch," Fetterman muttered, as if coaxing the projectile would help.

The rocket struck the diesel engine, cutting a hole in its side. The detonation rolled across the valley, reverberating off the tree line and echoing back. The locomotive rolled to a stop, a puny plume of smoke curling out of a jagged hole in its side.

Fetterman was disappointed that there had been no secondary explosion and eruption of flames, but consoled himself with the knowledge that the hit had obviously knocked out the engine for good.

Gerber spotted five NVA soldiers running along the tracks. The machine gun clattered as he riddled them with fire. All five flopped down onto the track bed, staining the gravel red.

The air inside the bunker smelled of gunpowder and hot brass. Fetterman started sneezing. Suddenly an RPG rocket whipped across the valley toward them. Instinctively Fetterman ducked, his hand protecting his head. The round slammed into the bunker with an earsplitting crash, and rubble pelted his back. After the dust thrown up by the explosion settled, he raised his head and looked across in time to see Gerber blinking with dust-rimmed eyes. Angrily the captain raked the hillside, trying to hit the man with the RPG. "Eat that, you motherfucker!"

A JAGGED BURST of machine gun fire shattered the silence. Umber and Roland watched in awe as red tracer bullets lazily arced their way toward the boxcars. Mouths gaping, they watched the fireworks from the top of the hill. They saw the boxcar self-destruct and then the steam locomotive. "Fetterman and Gerber" Roland said, sizing up the situation.

Umber seemed impatient. "When do we do our part?"

"Just hold on to your britches," Roland replied. "Fetterman told me I'd know when, and I will."

Roland was preoccupied. He studied the compound adjacent to the railyard where at least two hundred soldiers were filing out of the camp and filtering through the complex. Then they formed a skirmish line and advanced toward Gerber and Fetterman's position.

Roland pointed out one of the soldiers to Umber. "Look at what he's carrying. That's a Dragunov sniper rifle. Looks as if they intend to use a couple of snipers to pin down Gerber and Fetterman and keep 'em busy while the others try to flank them."

"I guess that means our time has come," Umber said gravely.

"Roger that," Roland said. "We're about to soak their asses in burning oil. Mind your eardrums. This is going to be one mother of an explosion."

Umber curled up in a ball, his hands protecting his head.

"Fire in the hole!" Roland shouted, detonating the set of fifteen charges.

Downrange, the C-4 transformed itself into white-hot gas that cut through the steel sides of the petroleum tanks like sabers through watermelons. The ruptured tanks spewed out gasoline, motor oil and diesel fuel onto the ground and downhill into the railyard. Some of the NVA soldiers were foolish enough to wade through the mess. Others kept their feet dry, but remained perilously close to annihilation.

Now it was Umber's turn. He pulled the pin on the M-26 fragmentation grenade and hurled it as far as he could, hoping it would land close enough to ignite the giant puddle. When the grenade exploded, earth and debris mushroomed into the sky. The resulting flames touched a trickle of gasoline and ignited it. In a few seconds a river of fire roared its way into the main pool of petroleum, creating a sea of flame.

Then, without warning, an RPG rocket landed in the middle of a large oil puddle. Obviously Gerber and Fetterman were contributing their two cents worth. The resulting explosion splattered burning liquid onto the enemy soldiers, setting them on fire.

Umber watched incredulously as enemy soldiers shrieked and tried frantically to douse their flaming bodies. Charred lumps that had once been human flopped in the inferno, wriggling like great beetles tossed into an immense barbecue pit.

The ocean of petroleum continued to burn a dirty yellow as black smoke wafted skyward. Soon the burning tidal wave of oil reached the line of boxcars, which burst into flame like so much kindling. Then, one by one, 82 mm mortar rounds, still wrapped in protective cardboard tubes, cooked off. The resulting explosions beat the already raging fire into a terrific frenzy. Entire boxcar doors and huge pieces of roof pinwheeled through the air, scattering deadly splinters in all directions.

By now the big machine gun in the bunker on the side of the hill had ceased fire. Roland figured that meant Gerber and Fetterman had headed for the assembly point. "Come on, Umber. Time for extraction."

"Wait a minute," Umber said. "I still haven't fired my rifle." He raised the AK to his shoulder and searched for a suitable target.

But when Roland heard a great rumbling, he knocked Umber to the ground and fell on top of him. A massive shock wave washed over them, and the intense heat burned the back of Roland's neck. The staff sergeant could hear chunks of metal and wood whistling overhead. After a few minutes, the two men struggled to their feet and looked down the hill. In the middle of the railyard was a new crater big enough to dump ten boxcars into.

"Come on, Davy Crocket," Roland yelled. "It's time to boogie on out of here." He grabbed Umber's arm and pulled the stunned man along with him.

14

NORTH OF IOWA CITY

Jody and Crystal left the city outskirts and began the drive to Monster's Christmas tree farm and the party. Laughing and giggling, they listened to a radio station playing the top hits of the week.

Down the road a piece, Jody spotted a pair of stationary taillights. Obviously another vehicle had stopped on the road, which prompted Jody to tap the brake pedal and downshift his Chevy to a crawl.

When he was close enough to view the situation, Jody saw a station wagon pulled over to the side of the road. Alongside the car, he could make out the dim outline of a man dragging something away from the center of the road.

As the road began a long, slow curve, Jody's headlights illuminated a man dragging a deer by its antlers.

Obviously the deer had been crossing the road when the man smacked into it. A moment later the Chevy's tires rolled over the blood-slicked asphalt.

"Oh, my God! Poor little deer," Crystal cried out.

When he passed the station wagon, Jody gunned the Chevy, fishtailing slightly as the tires slid over the deer's viscera. Accordingly Jody made a mental note to remember to slow down at this curve on his way back into town after the party so that he wouldn't lose control. Then he turned to Crystal and said, "This is a real bad section of road here on Highway 218. They call it Killer 218. Sometimes they call it Bloody 218. That's because of all the hairpin curves. And because of all the people who get killed trying to take them too fast."

Crystal's thoughts, however, were elsewhere. "Jody, what do you think about marital fidelity?"

"I don't know what you mean," he said. She had just dumped what amounted to a trick question on him, and he wasn't about to answer it until he knew what she was fishing for. As far as he was concerned, there was too much at stake. He wanted this woman desperately and he didn't want to screw things up by making a false move.

"Well," she purred. "I think a wife should be faithful to her husband, don't you?"

Jody followed her lead. "Oh, yes, of course." He was beginning to wish he had brought another woman to the party. The way things were going, he had a feeling he'd already blown his chance with Crystal.

"So you agree a woman should be faithful even if her husband is overseas and she hasn't had sex for a long time?"

"Yeah. Fidelity's important."

"So you believe in marital fidelity, then?"

"Oh, yeah, sure I do."

"Oh." Crystal fell silent.

Jody replayed the strange conversation and realized that she had just asked him what he thought about women who fooled around on their husbands. He gripped the steering wheel tighter, so angry at his own stupidity that his face turned red. Silently he cursed his own stupidity, and in desperation he searched for a way to save the situation, struggling not to blurt out something that would make things even worse. Finally he said, "Listen, Crystal. Yeah, I think you ought to be faithful to your husband. He's probably a good guy. If I met him, I'd probably like him. But a woman has needs. Desires. Some women are special, with special needs." He waited a moment before continuing, then said, "A woman like you is very special. Maybe you should be offered some kind of dispensation or something. Know what I mean?"

Crystal smiled and scooted across the long bench seat until she was leaning against him. "You do understand these things," she murmured. "I'd never want to hurt my husband's feelings."

"I understand," Jody said. "Discretion is important."

"Exactly."

"So I've been thinking," Jody said, "That if you ever decide to be unfaithful, I think you should do it with me."

"We'll see," she told him, patting him on the knee. "We'll see."

Jody pulled off the highway and drove down a short lane until he reached a parking lot. He and Crystal got out of the car and walked into the trees, homing in on the warm orange glow of a bonfire and the whooping and hollering of a hundred people having a good time.

Off to one side, a comfortable distance away from the bonfire, three long wooden tables held tubs of potato salad, barbecued pig, baked beans, hot dogs, hamburgers and corn on the cob. There were beer kegs everywhere, and Jody saw an enormous platter holding the skeleton of a turkey, its bones picked clean.

Out of the darkness someone called Jody's name. "Nice to see you could make it, Jody." Before he even turned, Jody knew that it was Monster. Everyone called the man Monster because of his great size. He stood nearly seven feet and was as broad-shouldered as an ox. Whenever Monster shook hands with you, your hand disappeared into a gargantuan paw. Yet despite the man's prodigious strength, he never intimidated anyone, whether friend or foe. He always gripped your hand as gently as if you were a frail, gray-haired grandmother.

Jody introduced Crystal to Monster and said, ''She's just a friend.'' Crystal and Monster exchanged pleasantries. She told him she was a poet and that she loved the country, especially the woods.

After eating some food, listening to a guitarist play some Bob Dylan tunes around the bonfire and watching a few couples make out, Jody leaned closer to Crystal, took her hand and noticed its warmth. Her pulse was racing wildly, her nostrils flared and her breathing had noticeably quickened. ''C'mon,'' he finally said, pulling her away from the crowd.

Jody led her to where the motorcycles were parked. ''Let me take you for a little ride. We'll take Rafe Tongue's bike. I've already cleared it with him.''

''This is a good night for a bike ride,'' she said. ''It's so hot. The ride will cool me off.''

Not if I can help it, Jody thought. Without another word, he threw a leg over the seat, reached down under the gas tank and flipped on the fuel switch. Twice he twisted the throttle grip, then stood up and threw his weight onto the kick starter. The exhaust popped once, then went dead. Jody twisted the throttle grip a couple of more times and fiddled with the choke. "Come on beast," he muttered under his breath.

This time when he kicked the starter, there was a pop, a rumble, then a roar as the engine caught. He twisted the throttle and revved up and down the rpm band until the engine ran smoothly. Satisfied with the way the bike was running, he let it idle. Then, grinning broadly, he motioned for Crystal to climb on.

Awkwardly she threw a leg over the seat and hoisted herself onto the bike, wrapping her arms around Jody in the process. Then she scooted forward on the banana seat, drawing herself so close to Jody that he could feel her nipples against his back.

He eased out the clutch and twisted the throttle grip so that the unmuffled exhaust roared. Once he was moving, he made sure he kept the engine revved as high as possible. The higher it revved, the more it vibrated the motorcycle frame, the seat and the riders, more particularly Crystal.

Jody bounced down a paved road, and despite the dirt and dust, Crystal enjoyed the cool wind blowing against her face. As the bike ate up the miles, she became more and more conscious of Jody's body vibrating against her crotch, massaging it as effectively as if he had his hand between her thighs.

Jody grinned. He could feel Crystal wriggling against him, working herself into a lather. When he figured she had enjoyed enough stimulation, he slowed the bike, pulled off the main road and headed down a gravel lane. Even though no words had been exchanged between them, she understood his intent and nuzzled her face against him with a familiarity as intimate as if they had known each other for years. Then she began to caress his stomach and slipped her fingers under the waistband of his pants.

Jody braked, revved the engine, then killed it. He threw his leg over the tank and took her hand, helping her off the bike. Even though she wasn't drunk, she seemed dizzy and unsure of her footing and laughed at her predicament.

They walked in silence down the path, hand in hand, until they came to a weathered building with huge double doors. Moonlight streamed through a window, illuminating a white stallion that whinnied at their approach and began to paw nervously at the oak floor planks.

Inside the building the air was thick with the sweet smell of freshly cut hay. Jody directed Crystal past the stalls to a wooden ladder that led to the hayloft. Once at the top, they picked a spot and lay down next to each other.

"I'm married," she reminded him, her tone hardly convincing.

Jody said nothing.

"I've never been unfaithful to my husband," she said. "Not even once. Although I'll admit I've been tempted."

Jody rolled onto his side and cupped one of Crystal's breasts. She responded to his move by stroking the hand manipulating her breast. Then taking his hand away, Jody leaned over and kissed her nipple, wetting the fabric of her blouse with his tongue and making the nipple stand erect. She moaned as he began to suck and kiss, then grabbed his hand and placed it on the other breast, showing him the precise caress she liked best.

Jody rolled on top of her and kissed her on the lips. Her mouth opened and she began to kiss him back deeply, her tongue laving his teeth. Jody's hand wandered to the inside of her thighs, his fingers stroking toward her panties.

She giggled and rolled him off her. "Undress me," she commanded.

Jody undid her blouse one button at a time. When the fabric fell away, she raised her arms and he pulled off the blouse. Taking a step back, he paused to drink in the curve of her breasts and the way her long blond hair spilled down her shoulders.

She unsnapped the brass button on her bell bottom jeans, then waited for Jody to complete the task. He leaned over and unzipped the pants, and Crystal hiked her hips so that he could tug the jeans off. He could smell her musky scent now that she was clad only in panties and bra.

"Make love to me," she told him. "Make love to me like you've never made love to a woman before." She held out her arms, inviting him. "Enter me," she moaned. "I want you in me now."

LATER, MUCH LATER, Jody returned the Harley-Davidson to the Christmas tree farm, then he and Crystal headed back to town in his Chevy.

As they drove, they could see fireworks lighting up the sky to the south above the city park. Jody shook his head. It was the same every Fourth of July in Iowa City. If he didn't hurry, he'd run into a massive traffic jam, the result of all the people leaving the park after the fireworks.

Jody gunned the Chevy as much as he dared, wishing the vehicle's headlights had more candlepower to illuminate the road in front of him. The straightaways weren't bad—the high beams were sufficient for them—but he was hitting the curves blind and that made him more **tha**n a little nervous. He probably should slow down, he told himself, but he never did.

He swore when the red flashing lights began to reflect off the rearview mirror. A moment too late he had seen the patrol car hidden in the shadows as he'd raced past. Without a moment's hesitation, Jody decided to outrun the cop. He stomped on the gas, and the Chevy lurched ahead. Glancing down at the speedometer, Jody saw that they were traveling over 110 miles per hour. The speed was no problem—the tires and shock absorbers were new.

But the flashing red lights stayed on his tail, so Jody goosed the engine even more. Still the red lights stayed with him.

Jody cursed. He knew he was in trouble. When he had zoomed past the patrol car, he had noticed it was a souped-up Chrysler Imperial. A baby like that could probably outrace him. And, sure enough, the big Chrysler was gaining on him. The police car was so close now that its flashing red lights dominated his rearview mirror.

Sweat beaded on Jody's forehead as he hunched over the steering wheel and stared straight ahead. He didn't dare look down at the speedometer; he was afraid to find out how fast he was going.

Crystal jumped up and down in her seat like a little girl at the circus. "Faster, Jody! Go faster!" she squealed.

Jody ignored her and watched the road. At that moment he saw a curve and a patch of red on the road that looked like someone had spilled a gallon of paint. Too late he remembered the deer that had been run over earlier in the evening.

"Faster! Faster!" Crystal shouted as the four-ply tires skidded on the asphalt.

Jody felt the tire treads break traction and the rear end of the car start to swerve. "I'm coming in too hot!" Jody screamed.

He swung the wheel violently in the opposite direction in a desperate attempt to correct the slide. For a moment it seemed as if they were going to make it. But then the car started to roll over onto its roof.

Crystal's squeals of pleasure became screams of terror. Upside down, Jody watched her face register sheer terror.

The Chevy was still moving, trailing sparks as it skidded along the pavement. Gasoline spilled out of the tank like a geyser until the car slid off the road and slammed into a tree.

Jody came to on the grass. He had been thrown clear, toppling out of the driver's door. He could see a pair of legs next to his left shoulder and wondered whose they were. He watched as a wall of flame followed a wet trail from the highway, across the shoulder and the grass and all the way over to his totaled car.

Then the Chevy started to burn. The fire was small at first, starting around the rear end. Then he heard moaning. Crystal was still in the car!

Suddenly the fire flared up, engulfing most of the Chevy. The moans turned into screams of terror. Straining to see, Jody saw that the passenger door was wrapped around the tree.

Jody tried to move in an effort to rescue Crystal, but he couldn't move. He looked at the pair of legs next to his shoulder and recognized his shoes. They were his legs, which meant his back had been broken and he was paralyzed.

Crystal shrieked, and off in the distance he could hear the dull pop of the fireworks exploding over the city park. At that moment Jody began to weep as he realized Crystal was going to burn to death and there was nothing he could do about it.

15

SON TAY RAILYARD

As the battle progressed, Gerber kept the machine gun going constantly, losing count of how many dozens of belts of 12.7 mm ammunition he had expended. As the gun continued to fire, it attracted more and more attention. That made sense, he thought. After all, they were the only targets the NVA had to focus on, so the enemy soldiers who weren't burning to death fired at the sandbagged bunker.

Bullets splattered the outside walls, tearing the sandbags to shreds. An unnerving number of bullets slammed in through the ports, causing Gerber to unfasten the machine gun's traversing mechanism. He crouched low so that no part of him was above the level of the gun itself. Then, hanging on to the trigger, he raked the ground below him, but was unable to see how effective his fire was.

A bullet burned the back of his neck, then another sliced the back of his hand. He stopped firing long enough to assess the damage. He felt the back of his neck. No blood. He looked at the back of his hand—just a scratch.

Gerber fired off a long burst that was interrupted as the machine gun jammed. He tried to work the bolt manually, but the fired round wouldn't extract.

"Case probably tore," Fetterman suggested. "Some of it's still lodged in the chamber."

Gerber swore, "I was afraid the gun was going to get too hot. Looks like we're out of business." He heard a commotion behind him and whirled around to see an NVA soldier standing in the doorway, his dark profile backlit by the sun.

Fetterman instinctively grabbed one of the AK-47s off the floor and fired from the hip. His first shot plugged the man in the head and chest, the impact knocking him backward out of sight.

Fearing there might be others lurking outside, Gerber threw a grenade out the door. It exploded with a tremendous roar, and they heard the screaming of two or more men as the white-hot fragments tore into their flesh. "Do unto others," Gerber said solemnly.

"Before they hurl a grenade unto you," Fetterman finished.

They could still hear screaming outside.

"We better finish them off," Gerber suggested.

"Before one of them finishes us off," Fetterman added.

This time the master sergeant threw the grenade. Once its roar diminished, there were no other sounds outside the bunker.

"Figure it's time to move on, Tony?" Gerber asked.

"Yes, sir. No time like the present." Fetterman hurriedly stacked six RPG rockets against the 12.7 machine gun and tripod. Then the two Green Berets left the bunker, jogging down the pathway toward the jungle. Once they were a hundred yards away, they stopped and turned around.

Fetterman sank to one knee and balanced the RPG launcher on his shoulder. He didn't waste any time getting the round off. The rocket whooshed, and a fraction of a second later, it flew straight through the doorway of the bunker.

The flat bang that emanated from within raised the roof about six inches before it dropped back down again. A great cloud of dust enveloped the bunker, but Gerber and Fetterman never saw it. They were already racing down the trail.

"The rockets were a good idea, Tony," Gerber said. "I was so anxious to hat up and move out that I forgot about disabling the machine gun."

Fetterman didn't answer.

"You, okay, Tony?" Gerber asked.

"Yeah."

"Well, what is it then? What's bothering you?"

Even though they were jogging and breathing hard, Fetterman sighed and said, "The steam locomotive, sir. It was beautiful. A work of art. I just wish we could have left it alone."

"I'd say that was the least of our worries right now," Gerber said, and they continued down the trail.

AFTER ROLAND FIRED OFF the explosive charges that unleashed a tidal wave of burning fuel, he and Umber leaped to their feet and took off. As they ran down the gravel road, the going was tough. Some of the chunks of gravel were the size of baseballs. A couple of times Roland's foot rolled the wrong way, causing him to falter and nearly sprain his ankle.

The two Green Berets rounded a bend in the road and immediately spotted a ZIL truck parked under the trees. Roland skidded to a stop, his heels kicking up a cloud of dust and gravel. Dodging over to the shoulder of the road, he ran headlong down the steep embankment, with Umber hot on his heels.

The two men threw themselves onto their bellies and waited for the inevitable hail of fire, but it never happened. They lay there listening. No firing pins clicked forward to ignite a primer, no weapons clattered on full-auto. There were no high-pitched Vietnamese voices directing a squad forward to flank their position. All they heard was the low, rumbling sound of a truck engine idling.

"What do you make of it, Henry?" Umber asked.

Roland looked at him, a little irked. "Call me Roland or call me Hank, but please don't call me Henry. I hate it."

Umber shrugged and grinned. "Sure, no problem, Hank. How about it, though? Why aren't they firing at us?"

Roland scratched his chin. "My guess is the truck's abandoned. Maybe when all the firing started the assholes took off for the hills."

Roland got to his feet, and Umber followed him. They sneaked along the shallow ditch that paralleled the road. In a few minutes they worked into position abreast of the truck.

Roland used hand motions to signal Umber to back away from the road and position himself closer to the tree line so that he had a better field of fire. Then the staff sergeant scurried up the side of the embankment and onto the road. Warily he walked toward the truck, holding his fire. Ten yards away, he paused to bend down and pick up a handful of gravel. Weapon held at the ready in his right hand, finger on the trigger, he started hurling rocks at the truck.

First he nailed the driver's door, chipping the paint. "Cheap Eastern Bloc metallurgy," he muttered. Next he hurled a series of rocks at the canvas sides covering the cargo bed.

When nothing happened, he yanked open the driver's door and stepped back, ready to cut loose with a full magazine if necessary. When he saw a human form dressed in khaki huddled behind the wheel, he instinctively let loose a 3-round burst. Before the flurry of bullets even tore into the man's chest, he realized that the driver was already dead.

Roland lowered his weapon and stared at the dead men whose throat had been neatly cut from ear to ear. A good deal of blood had puddled on the floorboards of the truck, already thickening like syrup.

The staff sergeant looked over his shoulder in Umber's direction and let out a low, barely audible whistle. Umber scurried up the embankment and across the shoulder until he stood next to his partner. He stared at the dead man dripping blood onto the floorboards. "You cut his throat, too?" he asked, slightly out of breath.

"Check the back of the truck," Roland ordered, his eyes darting everywhere, expecting a deadly fusillade at any moment.

Umber hurried to the back of the ZIL, hooked a boot in the tailgate stirrup and pulled himself up. About to swing over the tailgate and step onto the cargo bed, he froze, then yelled, "Hank, you'd better come and see this!"

Roland padded to the back of the ZIL and climbed up the tailgate to join his friend. He released a low whistle when he saw the cargo. "This what I think it is?"

"Yep," Umber said. "Dynamite."

Roland was pleased. "From the markings, I'd say it's Czech manufacture. Probably at least forty percent dynamite." He traced a finger along the black stenciling on the side of one of the boxes. "It's not Russian, Chinese or East German. That's for sure."

Roland squatted in the back of the truck. Even though he was shielded from the direct sun by the tarpaulin spread over the cargo bay, it was still hot. Overhead, the sun beat down with mind-numbing ferocity. It had to be well over a hundred. "Give me your Ka-bar," Roland said suddenly.

Umber furrowed his brow. "Why mine? Why not use your own?"

"Just give me your goddamn knife, okay?"

Umber unsnapped the leather strap that held down the knife handle, then pulled the long blade out of the sheath and handed it over butt first.

Roland worked quickly, prying open the lids of the wooden cases and exposing metal cans within. Next he grabbed the ring handle of the first tin and pulled hard, stripping back the metal from the hermetically sealed container as if it were a can of spam.

The sticks of dynamite glistened with nitroglycerin beads that had sweated through to the outside. There were so many beads that it looked as if it had been raining nitro.

"Truck's been sitting in the sun too long," Roland commented, wiping his shirtsleeve across his brow. "Ever work with dynamite?" he asked Umber.

Umber shook his head. "Had some cross-training back in Germany, but we only got to use C-4 and primer cord. Knocked down a stand of pine trees near the Black Forest once."

"Dynamite and C-4 are worlds apart. Dynamite's a different beast entirely." Roland skimmed off a couple of nitro droplets with his index finger and reverently whispered to Umber, "Got to be really careful when it gets like this." He flicked the fingerful of beads over the tailgate onto the dusty ground where they exploded with a loud snap.

Umber stared at the red dust disturbed by the mini-explosions. "Yeah, I remember. When it gets hot, the nitro gets so touchy you don't even need detonators to set it off. A well-placed bullet will kick it off."

"That's absolutely right. Nitro does funny things to your head, too. It passes through the pores of your skin and into your bloodstream and on to the brain. It can cause terrible headaches."

Umber nodded. "My guess is there's about a thousand pounds here."

"More like two thousand," Roland corrected. "All in half-pound sticks. Or whatever that works out to be in metric."

Umber hooked a thumb over his shoulder in the direction of the cab. "Who greased the driver?"

"Doesn't matter," Roland said, rolling one of the sticks of dynamite in his hand. "This is good stuff. We can use it. And the truck. Come on. I need your help. Let's yank the dead guy out from behind the steering wheel and get this rig turned around. I'm tired of walking, anyway."

But as they climbed out of the back of the truck, they heard a rustling in the nearby bush. AKs leveled, they crouched and turned to see what the noise was.

"Do not shoot!" a voice shouted. "It is Ngo."

"Who?" Roland demanded.

"Kit Carson. I am scout."

"Shit!" Umber muttered. "I can't see anything. Maybe it's one of Charlie's tricks."

Roland made sure the safety was off his AK. "We're out in the open. Why would they need to trick us?" Then, turning his attention to the bushes, he said, "If you're one of our Kit Carson scouts, come out with your hands high, real careful like."

After a moment or two, Ngo emerged from the jungle. He held an AK-47 over his head, his finger off the trigger.

"Sure enough," Umber said. "That's one of them."

"How do we know you're not NVA?" Roland asked suspiciously.

Ngo smiled, jerked a thumb at the driver in the cab of the truck and pulled out a wicked-looking knife. "He NVA. But no more. You like my work?"

"You did that?" Umber said, whistling.

Ngo nodded, then put his knife away. "We must hurry. No time to talk. Many enemy near."

"Let's take the truck," Roland said, moving toward it.

"No," Ngo cautioned, shaking his head. "Too dangerous. Many soldiers near. They shoot, we go boom. Must hurry now."

Just then a bullet slammed into the dirt near Roland's leg. "Holy shit, they're not near. They're here. Take cover!"

"You go," Ngo said. "I cover for you. Go now."

Roland stared at the man, the Kit Carson scout they had all distrusted so much. "You'll never make it. You'll—"

"Go now!" Ngo repeated more forcefully. "I pay them back for what they do to Nguyen."

"C'mon, Frank, let's hustle," Roland said. "We've got a date with Gerber and Fetterman." He clapped the tall Oriental on the back and then he and Umber slipped into the jungle. As they smashed their way through the thick vegetation, they could hear fierce autofire behind them. Ngo was sure giving the enemy a snootful of lead, Roland thought.

"Hey, Hank," Umber suddenly said as they bulled their way around a bamboo grove, "look at that!"

Lying on the jungle floor was a Dragunov sniper rifle.

"Maybe we can use this," Umber said, stooping to pick up the weapon.

"Yeah, sure, Frank. Next time we meet up with a tiger we'll be prepared. C'mon, shake a leg. Let's move."

Umber shouldered the Dragunov, and he and Roland continued on their way.

16

NEAR THE SON TAY RAILYARD

The NVA kept coming.

Roland resisted the overwhelming urge to fire off an entire magazine in one long burst. He resisted the temptation to hose down the area in front of him with bullets until his rifle was empty. He was well trained and knew that it was imperative he make each shot count. He knew that undisciplined troops often wasted their shots and then ran out of ammo in the middle of a firefight. In a live fire zone there were no time outs.

After he and Umber had met up with Gerber and Fetterman, the enemy had hit them with everything they had. Obviously Ngo had gone down fighting.

Roland knew someone would have to fight to the death here, too. He figured if Ngo could do it, he could do it, as well. The others would live; he alone would die. He started to chuckle. When he had been a little boy, he'd played Army with all the rest of the kids in the neighborhood until his teacher told him how a famous warrior named Roland had fought a delaying action for Charlemagne, king of the Franks, emperor of the Holy Roman Empire. And how Roland had valiantly died in the process to save his friends.

"We'd better make a run for it," Gerber called out to the team, breaking into Roland's reverie. "We can't hold 'em off much longer. There's too many of them."

"Go ahead," Roland said. "I'll cover you." He fired off a long burst as if to punctuate his offer. "I can give you covering fire for a few more minutes."

Gerber knew that if he allowed Roland to stay behind, it was a virtual death sentence. He also knew there was no other option. The sad fact was that one man would have to sacrifice his life or they would be wiped out to the last man.

The Special Forces captain looked at Roland sadly, then said, "Meet you at the extraction zone." He knew full well that no one would ever see the man alive again. Roland would earn his official CIB the hard way—with blood, all of it.

Roland grinned, then nodded at Gerber. "See you back at the helicopter. If I'm not there in ten minutes, go ahead and leave without me. I'll E and E to the coast or something."

Gerber reloaded a magazine and readied himself for the rush to freedom.

"Wait a minute," Roland called out.

"What?" Gerber asked.

"Your middle name isn't Charles by any chance, is it?"

"No." Gerber was puzzled by the strange question. "Why?"

"Never mind. It's not important."

Gerber, Fetterman and Umber crawled through the brush and into the trees. Once there, they took off as fast as they could, leaving Roland alone.

The staff sergeant fired a single shot at a group of three or four attackers who had crawled their way into position to attack en masse. The lead NVA soldier took the first round. It was as if the giant fist had angrily thumped him in the chest. The NVA did a double flip, landing flat on his back. Then he sat up, clutched his chest, got back onto his feet and took a few more tottering steps before collapsing to his knees, blood pouring from his mouth as he fell face forward into the dirt.

Roland kept firing, carefully picking his shots, making every round count. One NVA soldier hit by a bullet sat down hard as if he'd stepped on a banana peel. Sitting there with his legs splayed in front of him, he appeared to be oblivious to the bullets flying in both directions over his head. A bright crimson stain slowly spread across his stomach. Holding a hand against the bullet hole, he tried desperately to staunch the torrent of blood that gushed between his fingers. A moment later his chin dropped to his chest and he stopped breathing.

Roland's death-giving AK popped again, felling two more enemy soldiers. To Roland, it seemed as if the bullets passing overhead were the worst. Shattered pieces of leaves, twigs and branches rained down on him, and he was afraid that one of the slugs would clip him in the head at any moment.

Then it happened. He felt a bullet drill into him with a bone-crunching shock. The impact picked him up off his feet and hurled him backward onto the jungle floor, where he lay motionless, still holding on to the AK-47, his finger resting on the trigger.

Roland sensed that death was quite close. The world seemed to grow darker, and his breath became more labored. Still, even though his life was slipping away, he was surprised to discover that he wasn't bothered in the least.

He closed his eyes and strained his ears, trying to hear the movements of the enemy. After what seemed like an eternity, he heard a whisper and could faintly feel a man's footsteps nearby. There were two of them; he could now plainly hear their excited whispering. Although Roland didn't understand more than ten words of Vietnamese, he knew exactly what they were saying. They were discussing the same things he and his A-teams had dealt with whenever they had wiped out an opposing force. They were most likely wondering if he was dead, still leary of getting too close, afraid he might have some life left in him yet.

The talking finally stopped, and Roland sensed they were drawing nearer, one step at a time. He was pretty sure only two had been sent to check out his condition. They were in for a surprise, though. They were closer to death than he was.

One of the NVA troops tiptoed close enough to Roland so that he could smell the man's breath. When the NVA kicked the sole of his boot, Roland quickly made his move. Calmly he raised the AK-47 with one hand and pumped a round into the startled enemy. The man toppled backward as a bright crimson stain spread across the front of his khaki shirt.

The other soldier was so surprised that he dropped his AK. Roland fired again, hitting the man in the face, which exploded like a tomato.

Weak from loss of blood, Roland mumbled to himself, "Hasn't anyone ever told you guys to make sure the tiger's dead before you go kicking him in the ass? Too many hunters have been killed by a tiger they thought was dead." Having said that, he dropped the AK and once more closed his eyes. He was painfully aware of his labored breathing. His whole world seemed to be centered on forcing air into his lungs. Each breath was harder and harder to draw. He could taste his own blood and had to repress the urge to cough.

He knew blood was filling his lungs. He let his thoughts wander back to Panama, to Colón and the Club Trópico. To wonderful Anna, with her full lips painted red and her gorgeous body that set his blood on fire whenever she stood naked before him. Roland smiled one last time, then died, a full minute before an advancing NVA trooper fired a bullet into his brain to make sure, this time, that he was really dead.

The NVA soldier lowered himself to his haunches, grabbed Roland's chin and rolled the head to one side to get a clear look at the face. An American, Bicycle Chain Tran thought.

Then, as standard operating procedure dictated, he searched the American's body for ID cards, matchbooks, documents and maps, in short, anything that would provide intelligence data. But all Tran found was lint.

It was nearly the same story in the shirt pockets, with one exception. The American was carrying a cheap black ballpoint pen. Somehow the fragile writing implement had survived the hail of fire unscathed. Tran plucked it out of the dead man's pocket and studied it. He clicked the button repeatedly, first revealing, then hiding the nib. Finally, when he was bored playing with it, he stuck it into his own pocket and rejoined his comrades.

17

LZ WILD WILLY SOUTH
OF SON TAY

The landing zone was a small circle of grass barely forty yards in diameter and surrounded by tall trees. Gerber and his men huddled together at the edge of the LZ, where the helicopter would come to gather them up and deliver them to the relative safety of South Vietnam.

"You want I should call Frosty Ice on the single-side band?" Umber asked.

Gerber shook his head. "With the NVA hot on our tails, I don't want to use the radio if we don't have to. They may be monitoring, just hoping we key the mike so that they can run a DF on us and come running. No, I've got a better idea, a way we can maintain radio silence and still let the extraction team know we're here." Gerber slipped a small mirror out of his shirt pocket and pointed it at the sky, angling it so that the sun reflected off it. He tilted it back and forth so that its twinkling light could be seen from the air.

Fetterman impatiently checked his wristwatch, then squinted into the sun, searching the sky for any sign of the helicopter. "Where are the sons of bitches? Lost or just late?"

Gerber sighed, then stuffed the mirror back into his pocket. "Well, it was a good idea. Umber, you know what to do."

The radioman grabbed the mike and started talking in a clear, determined voice, as if the sheer intensity of his words would push through the airwaves and reach the pilot. "Frosty Ice, this is Frosty Shadow. Do you copy? Over."

Instantly the radio headset crackled. "Frosty Shadow, this is Frosty Ice."

"Thank God!" Gerber exclaimed.

"Frosty Ice, do you copy? Over."

"Loud and clear. How do you hear me?"

"Loud and clear. Frosty Ice. What is your ETA? Over."

"Ah, estimate three minutes to your location."

"Roger that," Umber said. "Standing by. Over."

The next two minutes passed by very slowly on the ground. It was as if time had stopped for Gerber and his men as they constantly looked over their shoulders, expecting to see a company of NVA advancing through the trees toward them.

Finally the radio crackled once more. "Ah, Frosty Shadow, we see what we think is the LZ, but we don't see you. Can you pop smoke?"

"Roger, roger. Will pop smoke. Over." Umber gave Gerber the go-ahead.

The Green Beret captain pulled the pin on the smoke grenade and hurled it. Hitting the ground, it bounced and rolled, then popped, releasing a thick red plume of smoke that trailed across the ground and marked their location.

"I ID red smoke," the radio crackled.

"Roger that," Umber said. "Red smoke."

"Get your hats and coats on, kiddies," the voice on the radio said. "We can't stay long."

Umber saw the aircraft first as the sun glinted off the Plexiglas windscreen. A moment later he recognized the unmistakable profile of a black Bell UH-1 helicopter.

"A Huey? What the fuck?" Fetterman blurted out. "How did they get a Huey this far north? It doesn't have the range even with auxiliary fuel tanks."

"I wonder why they didn't have SAR pick us up in a Sea Stallion," Gerber said.

Fetterman looked at the sky. "I've got it. Notice he came from the west."

"Laos," Gerber rasped, scowling.

If the Huey had come from Laos, that could mean only one thing: they were going back to Laos and some dirty little airstrip adjacent to a squalid little village. That meant it would be at least a couple of more days before they actually returned to Tan Son Nhut.

"Goddamn it, there's always something," Umber grumbled.

Then the helicopter was over the clearing and very nearly on the ground. The pilot flared, pulled pitch, and the skids touched down.

The rotor wash flattened the grass around the spike team members as they ducked and hurried to the waiting chopper. Gerber and Fetterman piled in first, and Umber had barely climbed aboard when the pilot pulled pitch and the aircraft took off. The procedure unnerved Umber when he saw how close the pilot came to the trees and when he noticed the rotor clipping leaves and small branches that got in its way.

"Tight LZ," Gerber explained.

In no time at all they climbed to a thousand feet. Then all three Americans looked down and saw the truck. None of them spoke. They just stared at the hordes of khaki-clad NVA troopers gathered around the ZIL with its cargo of dynamite. These were the men who had killed Roland, and Ngo.

"I hope one of those stupid bastards bumps the dynamite too hard and sets the whole works off," Umber muttered.

Fetterman looked at Gerber, then glanced at Umber's Dragunov sniper rifle.

Gerber grinned. "I know you too well, Tony. You're thinking what I'm thinking."

Fetterman nodded slowly. "You bet."

Both men stared at Umber's sniper rifle again. Finally Fetterman stuck out a hand. "Give me your rifle, Umber. I want to bang off a couple of rounds at the bad boys."

Umber grinned and handed him the rifle. Then Gerber talked with the crew chief, who relayed the message over the aircraft's intercom to the pilot. A moment later they started to hover.

"Here's one for Ngo," Fetterman murmured to himself as he slowly took up the slack in the trigger. Without warning, the gun barked. "Nice action," he said to no one in particular.

The bullet burned downrange toward the ZIL and ricocheted off the tailgate, chipping the paint and knocking a big dent in the metal. Through the scope the master sergeant watched in amusement as the NVA soldiers dived for cover. Fetterman worked the bolt, ejecting the spent shell casing and cranking a new round into the chamber.

This time he remembered to take a deep breath and let half of it out before squeezing the trigger. The rifle barked. A moment later he saw the bullet hit on of the wooden crates stacked in the back of the truck, knocking splinters everywhere. But the dynamite didn't explode. Exasperated, Fetterman cranked the bolt again.

Gerber offered words of encouragement. "Take your time, Tony. It's a difficult shot. It would be hard for anyone to make. But you can do it. Just pretend that's Jerry Maxwell down there you're shooting at."

Fetterman nodded, then relaxed. Letting out his breath, he squeezed the trigger. The firing pin clicked, but nothing else happened. Obviously, a dud. Quickly he cranked the bolt open and worked another round into the chamber.

"Here's one for Staff Sergeant Henry Roland," he said, then squeezed the trigger again. The gun barked, and a moment later a sharp white flash of light blotted out the truck. Shredded canvas, wooden bows and jagged pieces of metal wrenched from the ZIL flew out in all directions, cutting down trees and bushes. A cloud of dust obscured their vision, and a few moments later the shock wave buffeted the helicopter.

When the dust cleared, Fetterman could plainly see a gigantic crater gouged out of the red earth where the ZIL had once stood. All around the crater were further signs of devastation. A circle of trees closest to the blast had been turned into kindling, and a little beyond that the trees had been knocked flat, their limbs and branches sheared clean off.

"Jesus!" Umber exclaimed. "Looks like an A-bomb hit it."

"Right now there are a lot of NVA troopers playing handball with Stalin in hell," Fetterman said.

Gerber grinned. "Here's one situation where we can't get a body count. Closest we could come is a body part count."

BICYCLE CHAIN TRAN blinked twice. His ears ached as if nails had been driven through both eardrums. He could taste blood and dirt in his mouth. As he came to, he became aware of a horrible headache, and his back and shoulders felt as if a million needles had been pressed into the flesh.

He tried to get up, but found the task so difficult and clumsy that he lay back down. He called out to one of his comrades for help, but the sound of his own voice seemed far away and garbled as if he were talking underwater. He got onto his hands and knees and tried to get up once more. This time he was successful, but it was difficult to stand, the sensation not unlike those times at the Inn of Eternal Solitude when he'd been blind drunk and his sense of balance impaired.

Then he remembered the awful blast that had knocked him down and how he had thought they were under attack from B-52s, recalling the horrible sound and the deep trembling of the earth. For a moment he was confused and thought he was in South Vietnam. Then he looked down and saw that he was wearing an officer's uniform and remembered the battle he had just been in. He recalled the American soldier he had killed and the black ballpoint he'd taken from the body. Tran patted his hand against his pocket, feeling for the pen. Saddened, he opened his pocket and removed both pieces of the broken pen. Apparently, when he had fallen, he had landed on the pen and broken it.

Tran put his hands on his hips and looked skyward. He could faintly hear the beating of rotor blades and shielded his eyes to search the sky. Then he saw a black helicopter hightailing it for the Laotian border. "CIA," he muttered. "CIA dog soldiers."

Tran threw the remnants of the black ballpoint onto the ground, then crushed the plastic pieces to bits under his heel. Looking up at the sky again, he grinned. The Americans had won this time, but there was always tomorrow and the dark of night to protect him and his bicycle chain. Tran pulled the light blue officer-in-training tabs from the epaulets of his shirt and started walking toward the DMZ.

18

MACV HEADQUARTERS
SAIGON

Ever since the battle, the time spent in Laos, the helicopter flight to Tan Son Nhut and the jeep ride over the MACV Headquarters, the question had haunted Gerber: who were those guys at Son Tay. At first he'd only entertained vague suspicions, but when he was debriefed at MACV Headquarters by Jerry Maxwell, he was certain he knew the answer to the nagging question.

Maxwell handed Gerber a sheaf of infrared SR-71 photographs that plainly showed dozens of dead and mutilated bodies lying around the railyard at Son Tay. Gerber knew what it would be like on the ground, what the NVA relief troops would be experiencing. By now the air would be foul from the corpses that had bloated in the sun. The burned bodies would smell the worst.

The battlefield would be littered with the debris of war—bloody pith helmets and bullet-riddled AK stocks and canteens.

Gerber noted on the photos how the remains of burned-out railroad cars were strewn at crazy angles where rails had once been painstakingly laid. A series of huge craters dotted the terrain, as if a massive B-52 strike had annihilated the area. The infrared photography also showed that two days after Gerber had wreaked his special brand of destruction the petroleum tanks were still burning wildly out of control.

"Looks like a ghost town," Maxwell commented. "I'm glad you and Fetterman are on our side."

"Whose side are you on?" Fetterman muttered.

Gerber stared at Maxwell. "We're just lucky it turned out the way it did. Those extra troops the NVA had up their sleeve could have turned the tide in their favor. We were nothing short of real lucky. If they hadn't been so stupid with the way they located the fuel tanks so close to the railroad tracks . . ."

Maxwell cleared his throat. He didn't seem to have the nerve to return Gerber's gaze. Instead he busied himself with one of the photos, studying it intently. "Well, we're all counting our blessings that you made it back alive. You can be sure of that."

Gerber stood up. "Maxwell, you unprincipled son of a bitch. You knew all along they'd be there, didn't you?"

The CIA operative paused before answering, then said, "I don't know what you mean."

Gerber grabbed the photo out of Maxwell's hand. Then, in a slow, measured voice, he said, "I've figured it out, Jerry. Even in the heat of battle, in the short time we were at the target, it was obvious we weren't up against ragtag militia."

Maxwell sighed. "Okay, you got me. Again. Our intel was a little off."

Gerber chuckled, but he didn't find anything funny. "That was an officer training school, wasn't it?"

Maxwell nodded. "We had no way of knowing it would be the equivalent of the North Vietnamese army's West Point. We knew they had three other installations. How were we to know about the fourth? It must be brand-new."

"Yeah, it was damn unfortunate for us to stumble into that hornet's nest. Bloody miracle that we made it out alive," Gerber said, a sardonic glint in his eye.

"Yes. A miracle," Maxwell agreed. "We really should count our blessings on this one. I hate to lose a spike team."

"The CIA really fucked up on this one, huh, Maxwell?" Gerber said, menace in his voice.

The intelligence agent shrugged. "Guess we blew it big-time."

"No doubt," Gerber agreed, not smiling.

Fetterman watched in amazement as Gerber's face reddened and the veins stood out in his neck. The captain's fists were so tightly clenched that Fetterman wondered if his fingernails were going to pop off.

Gerber closed the distance between himself and Maxwell until he was leaning over the CIA agent's gray metal desk. Then, his voice cracking, the Special Forces captain, said, "Listen to me real good, Maxwell. I've spent three years running your spook missions in Southeast Asia. You don't care if you look stupid or incompetent to the Army, the Commies, the media or the general public. The only thing you CIA bureaucrats care about are results. Period. It's just like you guys to send us into an area of operations knowing full well it's the NVA West Point. You simply play ignorant, omit to tell us the important details. Then we infiltrate, make contact and the fun begins. We either live or die. Either way, we kill a bunch of their future officers and put a crimp in their war plans. No matter what happens, you win, and we lose."

Now it was Fetterman's turn. "Sentiments running the way they are back home, the American public would never approve of a raid into North Vietnam to wipe out a bunch of military types. But to blow up a strategic site like a railyard, that would be a noble cause."

Maxwell tried to speak, but all that came out was a hoarse croak. Then he tried again. "Like you said, obviously we fucked up."

For a while there was dead silence in the room as Gerber tried desperately to control his rage.

Finally Maxwell said in a feeble voice, "There's another issue you haven't considered."

"Oh," Gerber said, expecting to hear more lies.

Maxwell fidgeted with his tie. "There's a very important issue you haven't considered. One of extreme political consequence."

"And what's that?" Gerber asked warily.

Maxwell's voice was firm and focused, his eyes took on a deadly serious look and his voice betrayed the fact that he was very pleased with himself. "We got 'em real good last week." He hammered his fist on the table. "Yours wasn't the only mission we ran up there. I'm sure you're aware of that fact. Last week we ran twelve raids deep into North Vietnam. We struck with virtual impunity. And that, my friend, royally pissed off China. We have word that shortly after your raid on Son Tay, Peking sent a senior Chinese delegation to Hanoi to meet with North Vietnam's government. They wanted to review the situation. They expressed grave concern over how we're operating in their backyard."

"There's more, isn't there?" Gerber growled.

"Bet your military mind there's more. Red China's reconsidering their aid to North Vietnam." Maxwell whirled around to the filing cabinet, reached in and grabbed a handful of folders, which he promptly dropped. Swearing, he bent over and searched the file folders on the floor. When he found the one he was after, he snatched an SR-71 black-and-white glossy from it and handed the photo to Gerber. "I was about to hand this to you when you got bent out of shape. Look carefully. This is the Chinese border. Don't bother counting. There are a hundred railroad cars full of Soviet war matériel. They've been stuck there on the Chinese side of the border for days. Something about technical problems with the shipping documents."

Fetterman drew closer to Gerber and Maxwell. "So it doesn't take a diplomatic mind to figure out what the Chinese are up to."

"Yes," Maxwell said. "Until things are resolved, they closed the spigot on military aid to North Vietnam. Quite a coup for us, don't you think? So, are you satisfied, Mack? Does that take the edge off your temper? You know, you're a hero. Think of all the ground pounders' lives you've saved because the bullet that would have killed them is killing time in China instead of being dragged down the Ho Chi Minh Trail on some Cong's back."

Gerber inhaled sharply. "Jerry, you're never going to understand, are you? No matter how many times you fuck us up, you give us the same song and dance. For two cents, I'd—" Gerber's fist came dangerously close to connecting with Maxwell's jaw, but at the last moment the Green Beret captain managed to restrain himself. Instead, he said, "I hate that goddamn picture of yours." Saying that, the tore Maxwell's framed print of *The Hayfield Fight* off the wall and smashed it on the floor.

Maxwell's eyes almost popped out of his skull. "How... my... how could...?" he sputtered.

Gerber turned on his heel and stomped out of the office, while Fetterman glared at Maxwell. "Count yourself lucky that it was your picture and not your face, Jerry. Oh, and by the way, you still owe me a new Zippo."

The CIA agent opened his mouth to say something, but Fetterman walked out of the room, leaving Maxwell alone to brood about the drawbacks of life as an intelligence operative.

EPILOGUE

WILLOW VALLEY
CEMETERY IOWA CITY

Sergeant Frank Umber stood in the shadow of the monument at the foot of his wife's grave, smelling the unmistakable odor of freshly turned earth and listening to the birds singing in the trees.

Word of Crystal's death had been waiting for him in Nha Trang after the mission. As they always were in situations like this, the Army chaplain and the American Red Cross had been very helpful effecting emergency leave and transport back to the World.

Riding in the car from the Cedar Rapids airport to Iowa City, Umber had found himself amazed at the fields of green corn swaying gently in the breeze and the notion that he didn't have to worry about NVA lurking in the bush, waiting to put a bullet in his forehead. He didn't have to think about escape routes and probable direction of attacks from every new location he encountered. And even if his emergency leave wouldn't be a respite from emotional distress associated with his wife's death, at least he wouldn't have to worry about his own death.

Umber considered the age-old farmer's adage about the corn crop: knee high by the Fourth of July. The cornstalks were already standing waist-high, and it was obvious the farmers would harvest a bumper crop this season. He was glad he wouldn't have to look at rice paddies for at least the next week. In spite of his faithless wife's death, it was good to be back home again.

The night before, Crystal's family had held a wake at the Minner Funeral Home and, as usual, old man Minner wore his tasteless spade tie clip. Before the service, Umber had circulated among the crowd and overheard bits and pieces of conversation centered around Crystal's accident. It embarrassed him to find out that she had been with another man when she died.

Most of the people talking about the accident told it from the point of view of where they had been and what they were doing when Jody March had lost control of his Chevy.

A Hell's Angels biker type had arrived in the funeral home's parking lot on a Harley-Davidson and seemed to hold court in one corner of the room, away from the casket and the array of flowers.

"You could hear the ambulance and police cars coming for miles," he said reverently. "Seemed like it took 'em forever to get through all the traffic on Dubuque Street. The way I hear it, one of the paramedics had to get out of the ambulance and direct traffic so that they could get through. Goddamn fireworks! They ought to be outlawed among decent people."

"Bad accident," someone else said shaking his head.

"They burned, didn't they?" another asked.

"Yeah," the biker replied.

In a quiet voice one of the men said, "I hear you don't actually burn to death. You suffocate and your lungs burn out before you actually feel the flames." It was clear from his inflection that he was asking, not telling.

The biker shrugged. "Jody was thrown clear of the vehicle. He broke his back going through the windshield. Crystal was trapped in the car."

Angry at her obvious infidelity, Umber clenched his fists, thinking to himself, So you went out of this world with a whimper and a bang, eh, Crystal? He knew he should have been broken up about her death, but somehow he couldn't summon up the appropriate emotion.

And now Umber stood at her grave and reflected on how there had been a mild thunderstorm in the middle of the night that had cleansed the air of windblown dirt and pollen. Thick black mud lay where the grave diggers had shoveled up dirt from the six-feet-deep hole.

Umber didn't mind the familiar smell of the turned-up earth; it reminded him of foxholes and mortar pits. But the sickly sweet scent of all the flowers adorning first the funeral home and now the gravesite nauseated him.

Crystal's bronze casket rested on thick straps that would later be used to lower it into the ground. A bouquet of wildflowers had been strategically placed on the lid of the coffin. A tired old priest with whiskey on his breath droned on and on, sprinkling drops of holy water around the grave. A pink-faced altar boy, dressed in a surplice and cassock, followed in the priest's footsteps, spreading great clouds of sweet-smelling incense from a brass ball swinging at the end of a chain.

Close friends and relatives dabbed white handkerchiefs to their eyes, attempting to staunch the copious flow of tears. And then there were those relatives who had only turned up out of a sense of obligation, a kind of insurance for their own funerals, protection against being embarrassed by a dearth of attendees. These duty-bound funeral-goers stood impatiently in the background, wishing the ordeal would soon end so that they could go home and slip off their tight shoes and out-of-style suits.

Umber considered the situation. His beloved Crystal was dead. Poor, shattered Crystal, embalmed and laid out in a casket for eternity.

He was tortured by ambivalent feelings. In some ways he felt elated that Crystal was dead. She had been punished for her infidelity, her misdeeds. And yet he felt sad. His sense of loss was further exaggerated by the death of his comrade-in-arms, Staff Sergeant Roland. Umber cursed Crystal for dying, for daring to get herself killed at the same time as Roland. It seemed sacrilegious.

Finally Umber considered the irony of the situation. If Roland had been correct and Crystal had married him with the expectation that he would get killed in Vietnam and she would collect his ten-thousand-dollar life insurance policy, then everything was as it should be. Instead of her attending his funeral, he was standing over her grave with a check in his wallet from her life insurance.

Finally the priest finished his prayers, and he and the altar boy slowly walked to one of the cars, got in and started the short drive back to the rectory. The crowd started to disperse, and cars soon crunched over the gravel as they drove away.

Umber decided to stay at the grave for a while longer so that he could be alone with his thoughts. After that, he figured he would hit every bar in town.

Just then a young man with a red packsack stepped out of the dispersing crowd and walked directly toward Crystal's coffin—and Umber. The Green Beret sergeant thought he recognized the man from the poetry readings he and Crystal had attended. If he remembered correctly, his name was Larry or Bob or something like that. He was a high-strung sort with more than a few rough edges, as far as Umber could recall.

The young man rubbed the back of his hand across his eyes, sighed deeply, then placed his hand on the coffin lid and began to recite poetry in a low, melancholy voice, something about love and wine and dreams.

When he was finished with the recitation, he moved closer to Umber and said, ''You're Crystal's husband, aren't you?'' He extended a hand. ''We met at Kurt Donner's house, I believe. You know, the English professor who throws the parties after all the readings.''

Umber remembered Donner as the man who had mimicked the sound of Crystal's orgasms. ''Oh, yeah. I remember you. You're the guy who likes to play the cornet. The jazz man.''

The two men shook hands briefly.

''Terrible thing about her death,'' Larry mumbled.

Umber just nodded. There was really nothing to be said. Like it or not, Crystal was dead, and that was all there was to it.

Larry slipped off the red packsack, unzipped the flap and stuck his hand inside. A moment later he pulled out a .45 automatic.

Startled, Umber took a step back.

"Ever see one of these before?" Larry asked. "I suppose you have, being in the Army and all."

Umber nodded warily, his combat instincts on instant alert.

"I've been thinking about giving it to you," Larry said. "After all, you deserve it if anyone does."

Umber didn't like the tone of the kid's voice.

"I brought this one back from Nam. Killed dozens of Cong with it. Maybe when you go back to finish your tour, you could take it with you. You never know. It could save your life." Larry's eyes were almost popping out of his head now, and sweat beaded his chin.

Umber put his hands on his hips. "You did a tour in Vietnam?"

Larry blinked, then nodded.

"Oh, yeah, what branch?"

"Marines. Up on the DMZ. Did a lot of wet work. Behind-the-lines clandestine stuff, if you know what I mean. I'm the only guy who survived in my platoon."

Umber grunted noncommittally. "Yeah, I know what you mean. Things get pretty rough up there in Kontum Province. Five Corps is no fun. No fucking fun at all." Umber had cast the bait; now he would stand back and see if Larry took it. If he did, he would reel him in.

The kid squinted. "Yeah, Five Corps. Right there on the border of North Vietnam. They sent me there right after basic training. You had to learn fast or die. Most died young.''

Uh-huh, Umber thought to himself. Five Corps, up on the DMZ, not the Delta, and a Marine who went to basic training, not boot camp. He knew Larry was lying through his teeth.

The poet had become strangely silent. ''Yeah. I've killed plenty of men. Plenty, I can tell you.''

Umber wanted to shut the guy up—he was making a mockery of real soldiers, soldiers like Henry Roland— but the Green Beret knew better than to argue with someone holding a gun.

At that moment, though, something in the kid's eye told Umber he'd better make his move. Stepping forward, the Vietnam vet kneed Larry in the testicles and chopped him in the neck, relieving the stunned psychotic of the .45 in the process.

Larry, off balance, tumbled into Crystal's grave. Bewildered, he stared up at Umber. ''You don't believe me, do you?'' he croaked.

''Sure I do, kid,'' Umber said, smiling. ''I just wanted to see your pretty gun up close.'' He leveled the .45 at Larry's sweat-slick forehead, noting with relish how the guy's Adam's apple bobbed like the head of a chicken in a barnyard.

''W-what are you going to do?'' Larry squeaked.

"Do? Why I think I'll keep this fine gun of yours as a souvenir. Maybe you and Crystal would like to be alone." Saying that, he stuck the .45 into his service jacket, spun on his heel and walked away.

Umber had been wrong. The cornfields were filled with Cong. You could never let your guard down.

GLOSSARY

AC—Aircraft commander. The pilot in charge of the aircraft.

ADO—A-Detachment's area of operations.

AFVN—Armed Forces radio and television network in Vietnam. Army PFC Pat Sajak was probably the most memorable of AFVN's DJs with his loud and long, "GOOOOOOOOOOOOOD MORNing, Vietnam." The spinning Wheel of Fortune gives no clues about his whereabouts today.

AGGRESSOR FATIGUES—Black fatigues called aggressor fatigues because they are the color of the uniforms worn by the aggressors during war games in the World during training.

AIT—Advanced Individual Training. The school soldiers were sent to after Basic.

AK-47—Assault rifle normally used by the North Vietnamese and the Vietcong.

ANGRY109—AN-109—The radio used by the Special Forces for long-range communications.

AO—Area of Operations.

AO DAI—Long, dresslike garment, split up the sides and worn over pants.

AP—Air Police. The old designation for the guards on Air Force bases. Now referred to as security police.

AP ROUNDS—Armor-piercing ammunition.

APU—Auxiliary Power Unit. An outside source of power used to start aircraft engines.

ARC LIGHT—Term used for a B-52 bombing mission. Also known as heavy arty.

ARVN—Army of the Republic of Vietnam. A South Vietnamese soldier. Also known as Marvin Arvin.

ASA—Army Security Agency.

ASH AND TRASH—Refers to helicopter support missions that did not involve a direct combat role. They were hauling supplies, equipment, mail and all sorts of ash and trash.

AST—Control officer between the men in isolation and the outside world. He is responsible for taking care of all the problems.

AUTOVON—Army phone system that allows soldiers on base to call another base, bypassing the civilian phone system.

BDA—Bomb Damage Assessment. The official report on how well the bombing mission went.

BIG RED ONE—Nickname of the First Infantry Division. It came from the shoulder patch that contains a big, red number one.

BISCUIT—C-rations.

BODY COUNT—Number of enemy killed, wounded or captured during an operation. Used by Saigon and Washington as a means of measuring progress of the war.

BOOM-BOOM—Term used by the Vietnamese prostitutes in selling their product.

BOONDOGGLE—Any military operation that hasn't been completely thought out. An operation that is ridiculous.

BOONIE HATS—Soft cap worn by the grunt in the field when he wasn't wearing his steel pot.

BROWNING M-2—The 50-caliber machine gun manufactured by Browning.

BROWNING M-35—The automatic pistol, a 9 mm weapon, that became the favorite of the Special Forces.

BUSHMASTER—Jungle warfare expert or soldier skilled in jungle navigation. Also a large deadly snake not common to Vietnam but mighty tasty.

C AND C—Command Control aircraft that circled overhead to direct the combined air and ground operations.

CAO BOIS—(cowboys) Term that referred to the criminals of Saigon who rode motorcycles.

CARIBOU—Cargo transport plane.

CHICOM—Chinese Communist. Troops or weapons and equipment supplied by Red China.

CHINOOK—Army Aviation twin-engine helicopter. A CH-47. Also known as a SHIT HOOK.

CHOCK—Refers to the number of the aircraft in flight. Chock Three is the third, Chock Six is the sixth.

CLAYMORE—Antipersonnel mine that fires seven hundred and fifty steel balls with a lethal range of fifty meters.

CLOSE AIR SUPPORT—Use of airplanes and helicopters to fire on enemy units near friendly troops.

CO CONG—Female Vietcong.

COLT—Soviet-built small transport plane. The NATO code name for Soviet and Warsaw Pact transport planes all begin with the letter C.

COMSEC—Communications security.

CONEX—Steel container about ten feet high, ten feet deep and ten feet long used to haul equipment and supplies.

CS—A persistent form of improved tear gas (usually dispersed as a fine powder from grenades) used as a military and riot control agent.

DAC CONG—Sappers who attack in the front ranks to blow up the wire so that the infantry can assault the camp.

DAI UY—Vietnamese army rank, the equivalent of captain.

DEROS—Date of estimated return from overseas.

DIRNSA—Director, National Security Agency.

E AND E—Escape and Evasion.

FEET WET—Terms used by pilots to describe flight over water.

FIELD GRADE—Refers to officers above the rank of captain but under that of brigadier general. In other words, majors, lieutenant colonels and colonels.

FIRECRACKER—Special artillery shell that explodes into a number of small bomblets to detonate later. It is the artillery version of the cluster bomb and was a secret weapon employed tactically for the first time at Khe Sanh.

FIRST SHIRT—First Sergeant.

FIVE—Radio call sign for the executive officer of a unit.

FNG—Fucking new guy.

FOB—Forward operating base.

FOX MIKE—FM radio.

FREEDOM BIRD—Name given to any aircraft that took troops out of Vietnam. Usually referred to as the commercial jet flights that took men back to the World.

GARAND—The M-1 rifle that was replaced by the M-14. Issued to the Vietnamese early in the war.

GO-TO-HELL RAG—Towel or any large cloth worn around the neck by grunts.

GRAIL—NATO name for the shoulder-fired SA-7 surface-to-air missile.

GUARD THE RADIO—Stand by in the commo bunker and listen for messages.

GUIDELINE—NATO name for the SAs surface-to-air missle.

GUNSHIP—Armed helicopter or cargo plane that carries weapons instead of cargo.

HE—High-explosive ammunition.

HOOTCH—Almost any shelter, from temporary to long-term.

HORN—Term referring to a specific kind of radio operations that used satellites to rebroadcast the messages.

HORSE—See BISCUIT.

HOTEL THREE—Helicopter landing area at Saigon's Tan Son Nhut Airport.

HUEY—UH-1 helicopter.

HUMINT—Human Intelligence resources. In other words, they talked to someone who gave them the information.

ICS—Official name of the intercom system in an aircraft.

IN-COUNTRY—Term used to refer to American troops operating in South Vietnam. They were all in-country.

INTELLIGENCE—Any information about enemy operations. It can include troop movements, weapons capabilities, biographies of enemy commanders and general information about terrain features. Any information that would be useful in planning a mission.

KA-BAR—Type of military combat knife.

KIA—Killed in action. (Since the US was not engaged in a declared war, the use of the term KIA was not authorized. KIA came to mean enemy dead. Americans were KHA—killed in hostile action).

KLICK—A thousand meters. A kilometer.

LIMA LIMA—Land line. Refers to telephone communications between two points on the ground.

LLDB—Luc Luong Dac Biet. The South Vietnamese Special Forces. Sometimes referred to as the Look Long, Duck Back.

LP—Listening Post. A position outside the perimeter manned by a couple of soldiers to give advance warning of enemy activity.

LRRP—Long-range Reconnaissance Patrol.

LSA—Lubricant used by soldiers on their weapons to ensure they will continue to operate properly.

LZ—Landing zone.

M-3A1—Also known as a grease gun. A .45-caliber submachine gun favored in World War Two by the GIs because its slow rate of fire meant that the barrel didn't rise and they didn't burn through their ammo as fast as they did with some other weapons.

M-14—Standard rifle of the U.S. Army, eventually replaced by the M-16. It fired the standard NATO round—7.62 mm.

M-16—Standard infantry weapon of the Vietnam War. It fired the 5.56 mm ammunition.

M-79—Short-barrel shoulder-fired weapon that fires a 40 mm grenade. These can be high explosives, white phosphorus or canister.

M-113—Numerical designation of an armored personnel carrier.

MACV—Military Assistance Command, Vietnam, replaced MAAG in 1964.

MAD MINUTE—A specified time on a base camp when the men in the bunkers would clear their weapons. It came to mean the random firing of the camp's weapons just as fast as everyone could shoot.

MATCU—Marine Air Traffic Control Unit.

MEDEVAC—Also called Dustoff. Helicopter used to take the wounded to medical facilities.

MI—Military intelligence.

MIA—Missing in action.

MONOPOLY MONEY—A term used by the servicemen in Vietnam to describe the MPC handed out in lieu of regular U.S. currency.

MOS—Military Occupation Specialty. It is a job description.

MPC—Military Payment Certificates. The monopoly money used instead of real cash.

NCO—A noncommissioned officer. A noncom. A sergeant.

NCOIC—NCO in charge. The senior NCO in a unit, detachment or patrol.

NDB—Nondirectional beacon. A radio beacon that can be used for homing.

NEXT—The man who was the next to be rotated home. See SHORT.

NINETEEN—The average age of the combat soldier in Vietnam, as opposed to twenty-six in World War II.

NOUC MAM—A foul-smelling sauce used by the Vietnamese.

NVA—The North Vietnamese Army. Also used to designate a soldier from North Vietnam.

ONTOS—A Marine weapon that consists of six 106 mm recoilless rifles mounted on a tracked vehicle.

ORDER OF BATTLE—A listing of the units available and to be used during the battle. It is not necessarily a list of how or when the units will be used, but a listing of who and what could be used.

P (PIASTER)—The basic monetary unit in South Vietnam, worth slightly less than a penny.

PETA-PRIME—Tarlike substance that melted in the heat of the day to become a sticky black nightmare that clung to boots, clothes and equipment. It was used to hold down the dust during the dry season.

PETER PILOT—The copilot in a helicopter.

PLF—Parachute landing fall. The roll used by parachutists on landing.

POL—Petroleum, oil and lubricants. The refueling point on many military bases.

POW—Prisoner of war.

PRC-10—Portable radio.

PRC-25—A lighter portable radio that replaced the PRC-10.

PULL PITCH—Term used by helicopter pilots that means they are going to take off.

PUNJI STAKE—Sharpened bamboo hidden to penetrate the foot, sometimes dipped in feces.

PUZZLE PALACE—A term referring to the Pentagon. It was called the puzzle palace because no one knew what was going on in it. The Puzzle Palace East referred to MACV or USARV Headquarters in Saigon.

RED LEGS—A term that refers to the artillerymen. It comes from the old Army where the artillerymen wore a red stripe on the legs of their uniforms.

REMF—A rear-echelon motherfucker.

RINGKNOCKER—Graduate of a military academy. The terms refers to the ring worn by all graduates.

RON—Remain Overnight. Term used by flight crews to indicate a flight that would last longer than a day.

RPD—Soviet-made light machine gun, 7.62 mm.

RTO—Radio telephone operator. The radio man of a unit.

RUFF-PUFFS—A term applied to the RF-PFs, the regional forces and popular forces. Militia drawn from the local population.

S-3—The company-level operations officer. He is the same as the G-3 on a general's staff.

SA-2—A surface-to-air missile fired from a fixed site. It is a radar-guided missile nearly thirty-five feet long.

SA-7—A surface-to-air missile that is shoulder-fired and infrared homing.

SACSA—Special Assistant for Counterinsurgency and Special Activities.

SAFE AREA—Selected area for evasion. It doesn't mean that the area is safe from the enemy, only that the terrain, location or local population make the area a good place for escape and evasion.

SAM TWO—A reference to the SA-2 Guideline.

SAR—Search and rescue. SAR forces are the people involved in search and rescue missions.

SECDEF—Secretary of Defense.

SHORT-TIME—A GI term for a quickie.

SHORT-TIMER—Person who had been in Vietnam for nearly a year and who would be rotated back to the World soon. When his DEROS was the shortest in the unit, the person was said to be next.

SINGLE DIGIT MIDGET—A soldier with fewer than ten days left in-country.

SIX—Radio call sign for the unit commander.

SKS—Soviet-made carbine.

SMG—Submachine gun.

SOG—Studies and Observations Group. Cover name used for MACV Special Operations.

SOI—Signal operating instructions. The booklet that contained the call signs and radio frequencies of the units in Vietnam.

SOP—Standard operating procedure.

SPIKE TEAM—Special Forces team made up for a direct action mission.

STEEL POT—The standard U.S Army helmet. The steel pot was the outer metal cover.

TAOR—Tactical area of operation responsibility.

TEAM UNIFORM OR COMPANY UNIFORM—UHF radio frequency on which the team or the company communicates. Frequencies were changed periodically in an attempt to confuse the enemy.

THE WORLD—The United States.

THREE—Radio call sign of the operations officer.

THREE CORPS—The military area around Saigon. Vietnam was divided into four corps areas.

TOC—Tactical operations center.

TO&E—Table of organization and equipment. A detailed listing of all the men and equipment assigned to a unit.

TOT—Time over target. It refers to the time that the aircraft are supposed to be over the drop zone with the parachutists, or the target if the planes are bombers.

TRICK CHIEF—NCOIC for a shift.

TRIPLE A—Antiaircraft Artillery or AAA. Anything used to shoot at airplanes and helicopters.

TWO—Radio call sign of the Intelligence officer.

TWO-OH-ONE (201) FILE—The military records file that listed all a soldier's qualifications, training, experience and abilities. It was passed from unit to unit so that the new commander would have some idea about the capabilities of the incoming soldier.

UMZ—Ultramilitarized zone, the name GIs gave to the DMZ (DeMilitarized Zone).

UNIFORM—Refers to UHF radio. Company Uniform would be the frequency assigned to that company.

URC-10—A small emergency communications radio used by Special Forces LRRPs.

USARV—United States Army, Vietnam.

VC—Vietcong, called Victor Charlie (phonetic alphabet) or just Charlie.

VIETCONG—A contraction of Vietnam Cong San (Vietnamese Communist).

VIET CONG SAN—The Vietnamese Communists. A term in use since 1956.

WHITE MICE—Refers to the South Vietnamese military police because they all wore white helmets.

WIA—Wounded in action.

WILLIE PETE—WP, white phosphorus, called smoke rounds. Also used as antipersonnel weapons.

WSO—Weapons system officer. The name given to the man who rode in the back seat of a Phantom because he was responsible for the weapons systems.

XO—Executive officer of a unit.

X-RAY—A term that refers to an engineer assigned to a unit.

ZAP—To ding, pop caps or shoot. To kill.

**Able Team battles a Vietnamese drug network
in Southern California.**

SUPER ABLE TEAM #2

HOSTILE FIRE

DICK STIVERS

A South Vietnamese heroin network, so powerful during the
Vietnam War, is still intact, and this time they're doing business in
the U.S. The Black Ghosts, led by a former VC general, are growing
strong in Southern California and for good reason—they have special CIA training.

It's a situation that's making Able Team see red—and they're making it their mission to stop the communist presence from infiltrating California.

DON PENDLETON's

MACK BOLAN.

Backlash

Mack Bolan kicks open a hornet's nest when he discovers a Nicaraguan power monger has been running drugs off the coast of Miami to finance an overthrow of the Sandinista regime...and has had a lot of help from the CIA.

Now the Company wants out and calls on the one man who can salvage this operation gone haywire...THE EXECUTIONER!

Do you know a real hero?

At Gold Eagle Books we know that heroes are not just fictional. Everyday someone somewhere is performing a selfless task, risking his or her own life without expectation of reward.

Gold Eagle would like to recognize America's local heroes by publishing their stories. If you know a true to life hero (that person might even be you) we'd like to hear about him or her. In 150-200 words tell us about a heroic deed you witnessed or experienced. Once a month, we'll select a local hero and award him or her with national recognition by printing his or her story on the inside back cover of THE EXECUTIONER series, and the ABLE TEAM, PHOENIX FORCE and/or VIETNAM: GROUND ZERO series.

Send your name, address, zip or postal code, along with your story of 150-200 words (and a photograph of the hero if possible), and mail to:

LOCAL HEROES AWARD
Gold Eagle Books
225 Duncan Mill Road
Don Mills, Ontario
M3B 3K9
Canada

The following rules apply: All stories and photographs submitted to Gold Eagle Books, published or not, become the property of Gold Eagle and cannot be returned. Submissions are subject to verification by local media before publication can occur. Not all stories will be published and photographs may or may not be used. Gold Eagle reserves the right to reprint an earlier LOCAL HEROES AWARD in the event that a verified hero cannot be found. Permission by the featured hero must be granted in writing to Gold Eagle Books prior to publication. Submit entries by December 31, 1990.

HERO-1R